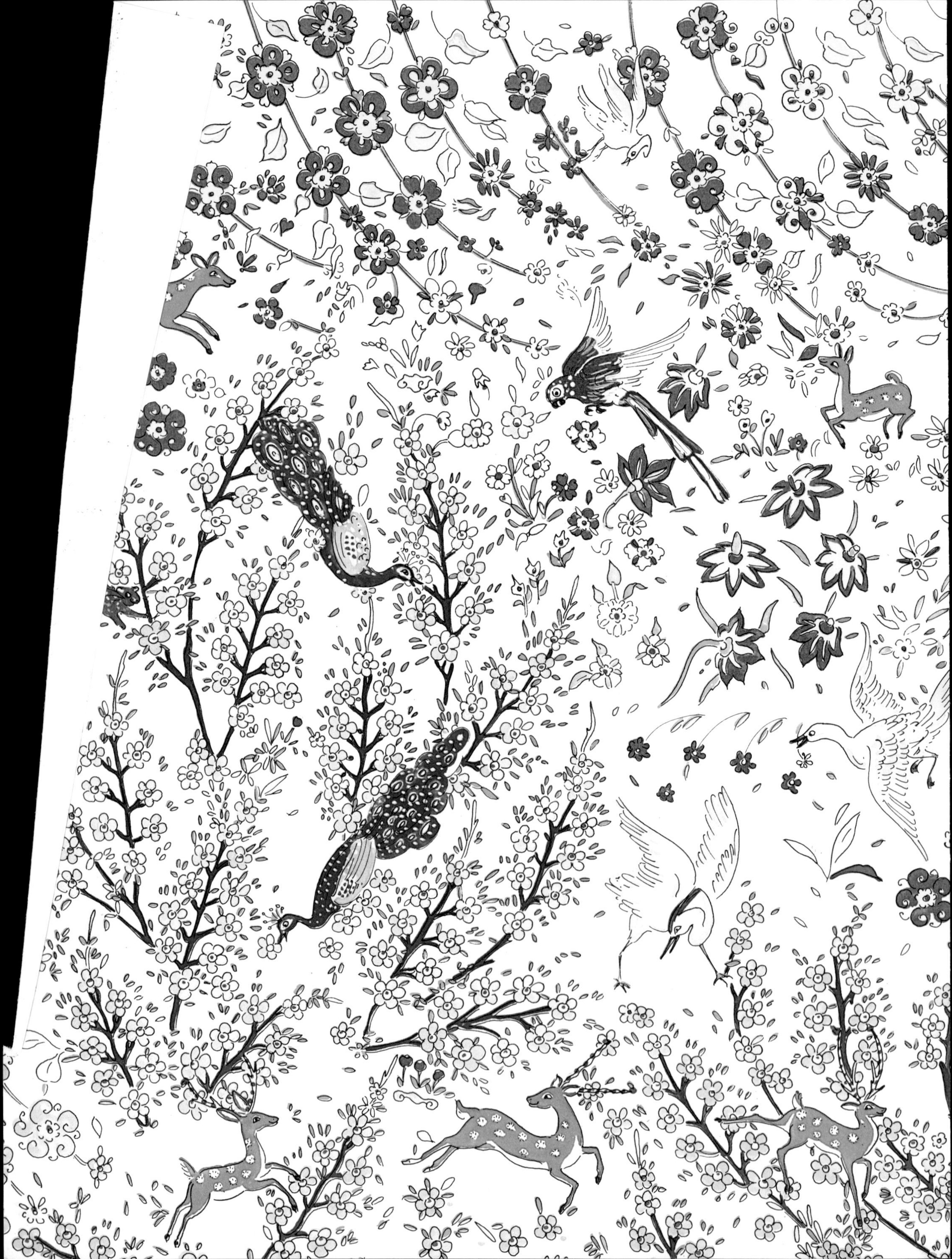

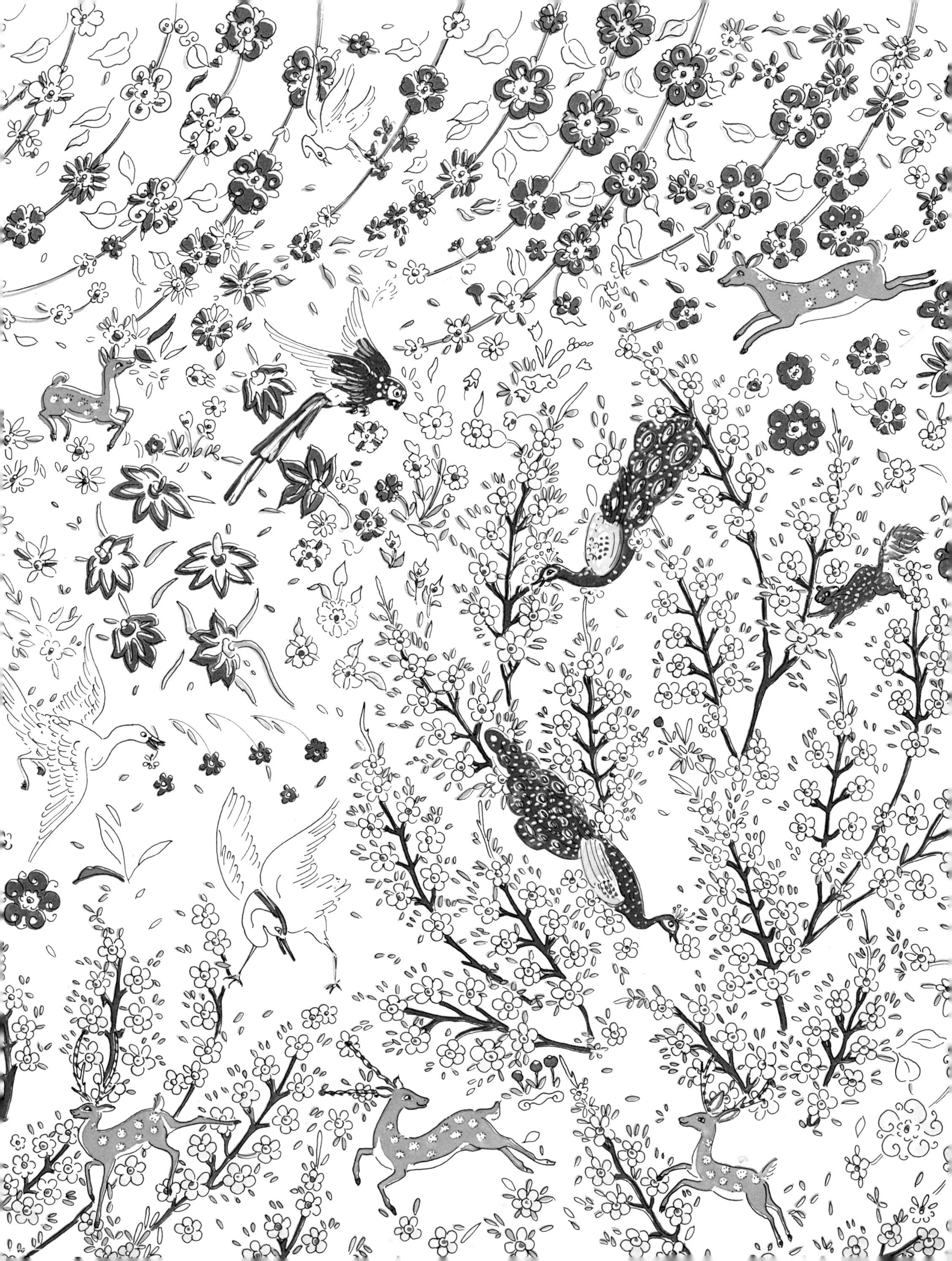

FAT GOPAL

BY

Jacquelin Singh

ILLUSTRATED BY

Demi

HARCOURT BRACE JOVANOVICH, PUBLISHERS

SAN DIEGO   NEW YORK   LONDON

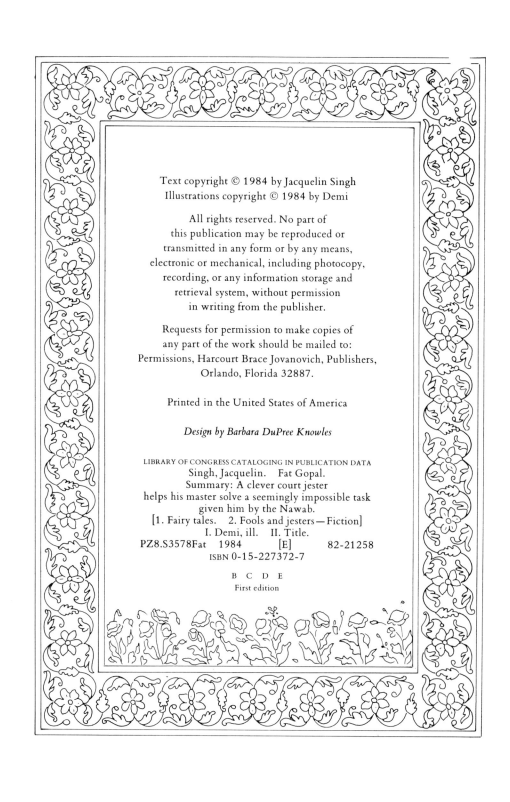

Printed in the United States of America

Design by Barbara DuPree Knowles

LIBRARY OF CONGRESS CATALOGING IN PUBLICATION DATA
Singh, Jacquelin.   Fat Gopal.
Summary: A clever court jester
helps his master solve a seemingly impossible task
given him by the Nawab.
[1. Fairy tales.   2. Fools and jesters—Fiction]
I. Demi, ill.   II. Title.
PZ8.S3578Fat   1984   [E]   82-21258
ISBN 0-15-227372-7

B   C   D   E
First edition

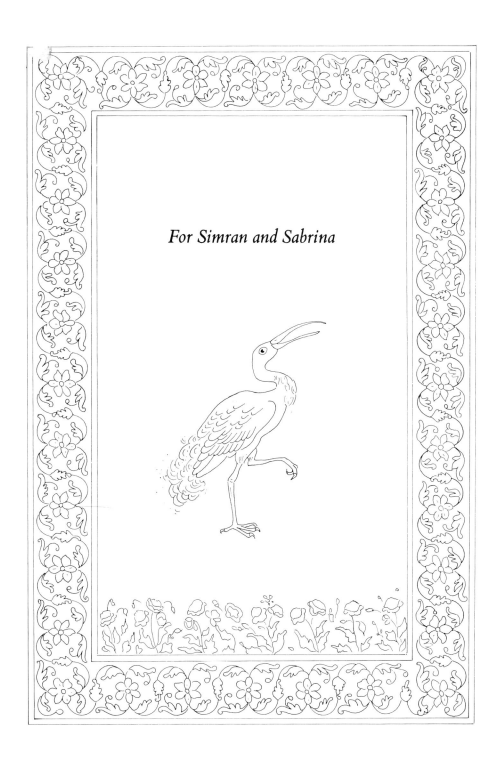

For Simran and Sabrina

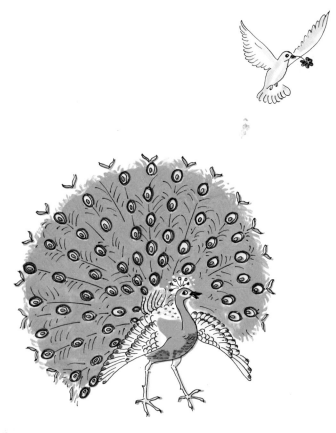

There once was a Nawab who ruled all the land between the mountains and the sea. His palace stood in the center of a big courtyard.

Every day people from all over the kingdom gathered to meet him. While they waited, they sat on cushions fanning themselves and were entertained by the peacocks talking to one another in the trees, by monkeys stealing honey from the beehives, and by girls dancing in a row, arm in arm.

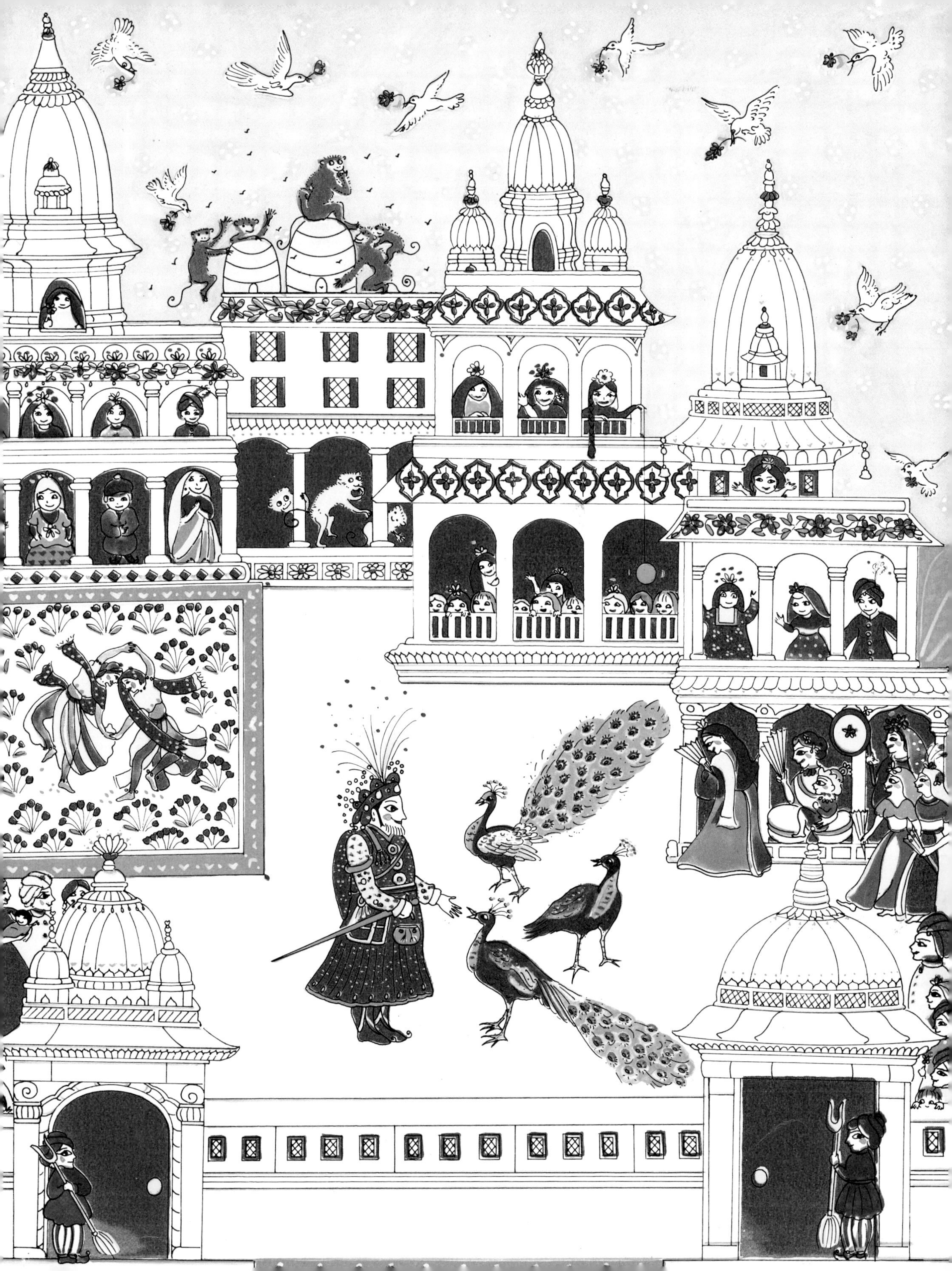

One day a Maharajah, who ruled over a small kingdom within this land, said, "I must go visit the Nawab and pay my respects."

He rode to the Nawab's palace on an elephant. Musicians marched behind him. On a funny-looking horse was the court jester, Fat Gopal, whose job it was to make everybody laugh. Servants carried presents for the Nawab: baskets of bananas and pineapples and oranges on their heads and buckets of honey on poles across their shoulders.

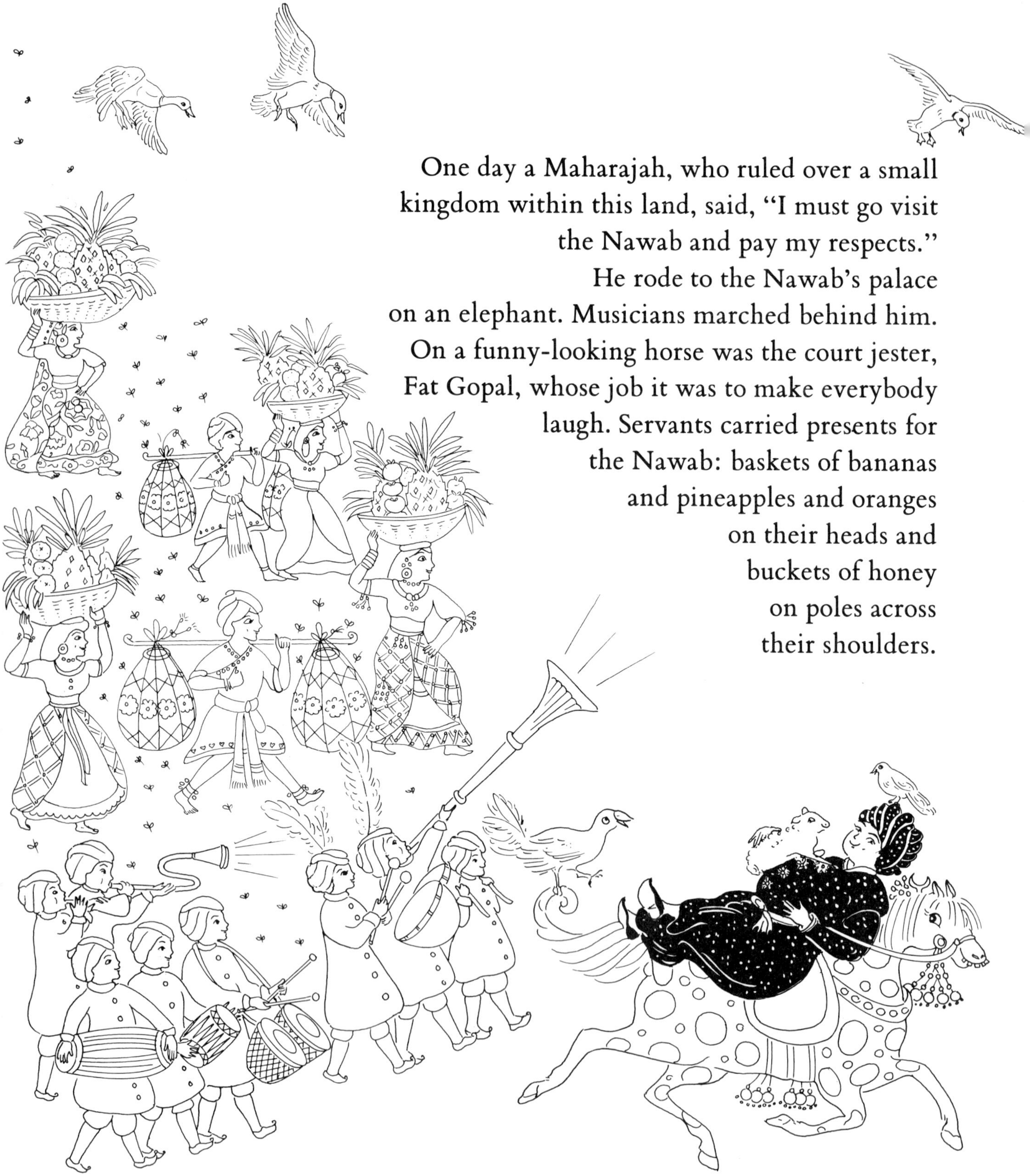

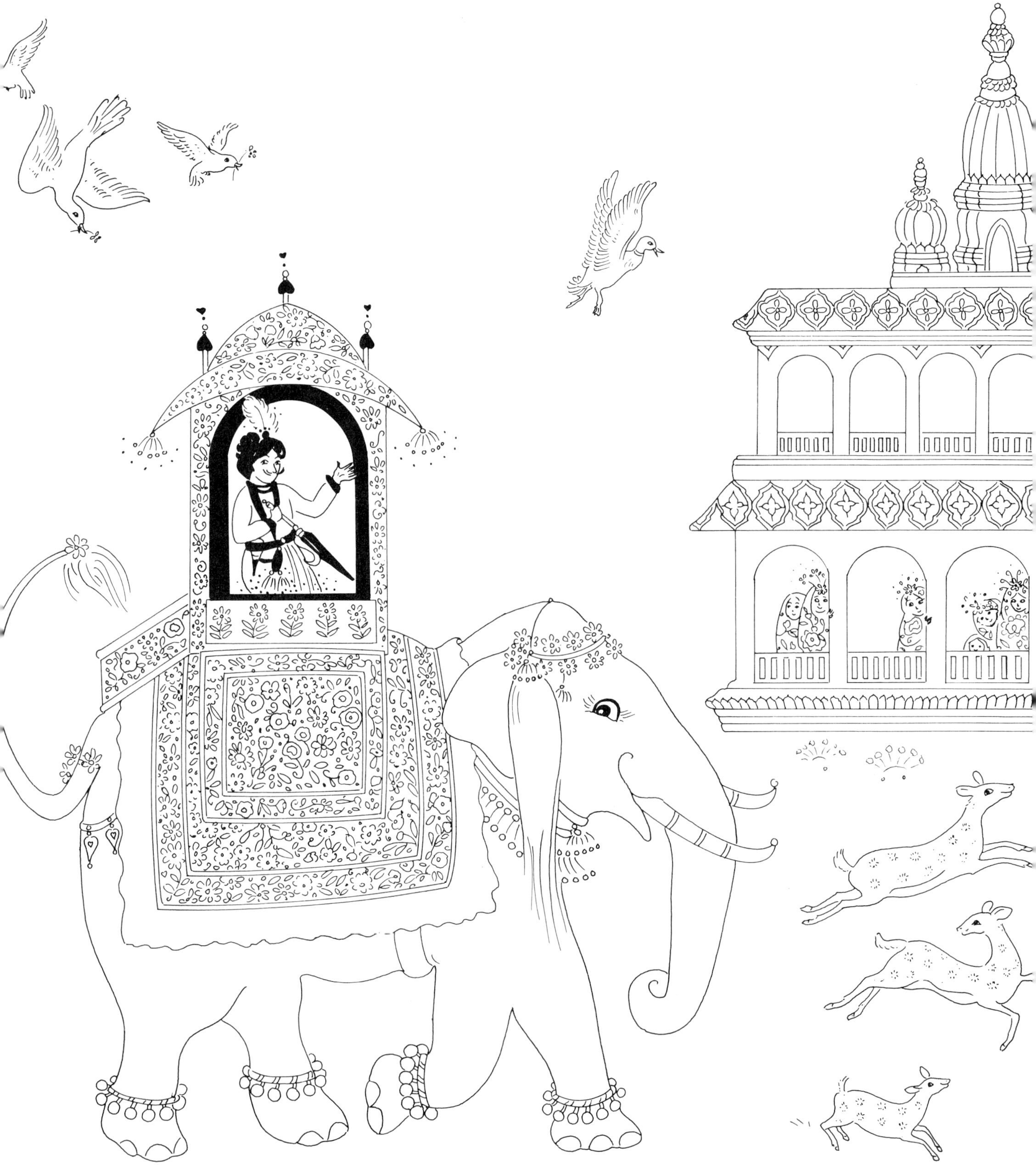

During the Maharajah's visit, the Nawab laughed at Fat Gopal's jokes and enjoyed the music. He said the presents were all right too. But he wanted the Maharajah to do something more for him.

"Come out here," he said, leading the Maharajah to a balcony. When they got outside, the Nawab pointed to where the land and sky met. "I want the whole earth measured from side to side and from top to bottom." Then he spread his arms wide toward the sky. "I also want you to count all the stars."

The Maharajah opened his mouth to speak, but before he could say anything, the Nawab went on. "While you're at it, you might as well find out how many rays the sun has and how many men there are in the moon."

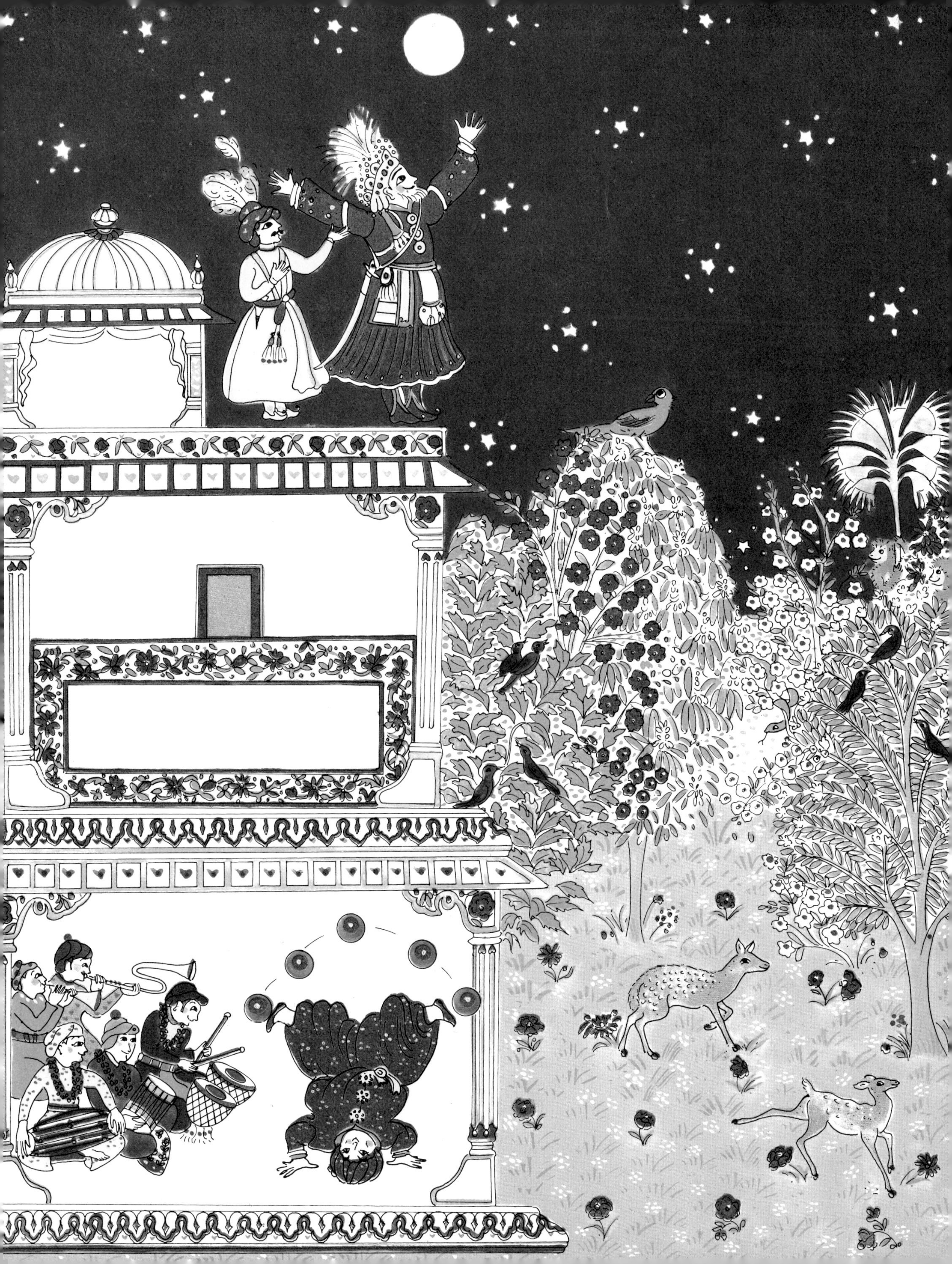

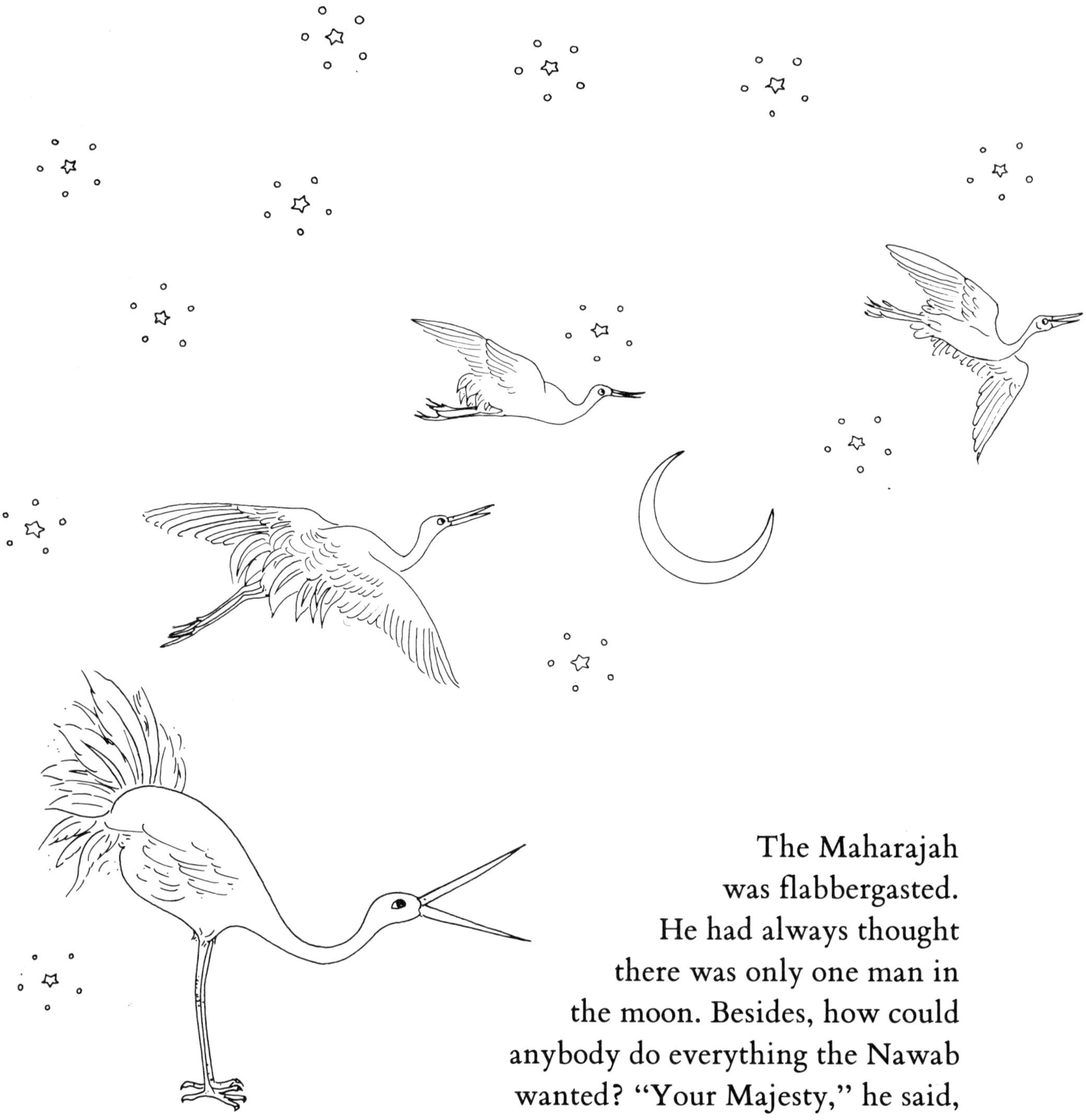

The Maharajah
was flabbergasted.
He had always thought
there was only one man in
the moon. Besides, how could
anybody do everything the Nawab
wanted? "Your Majesty," he said,
"I'd like to do just as you wish, but you've
asked me to do the impossible and . . ."
"And that's exactly what you'll
do," the Nawab said, "if you don't want
to lose your head!"

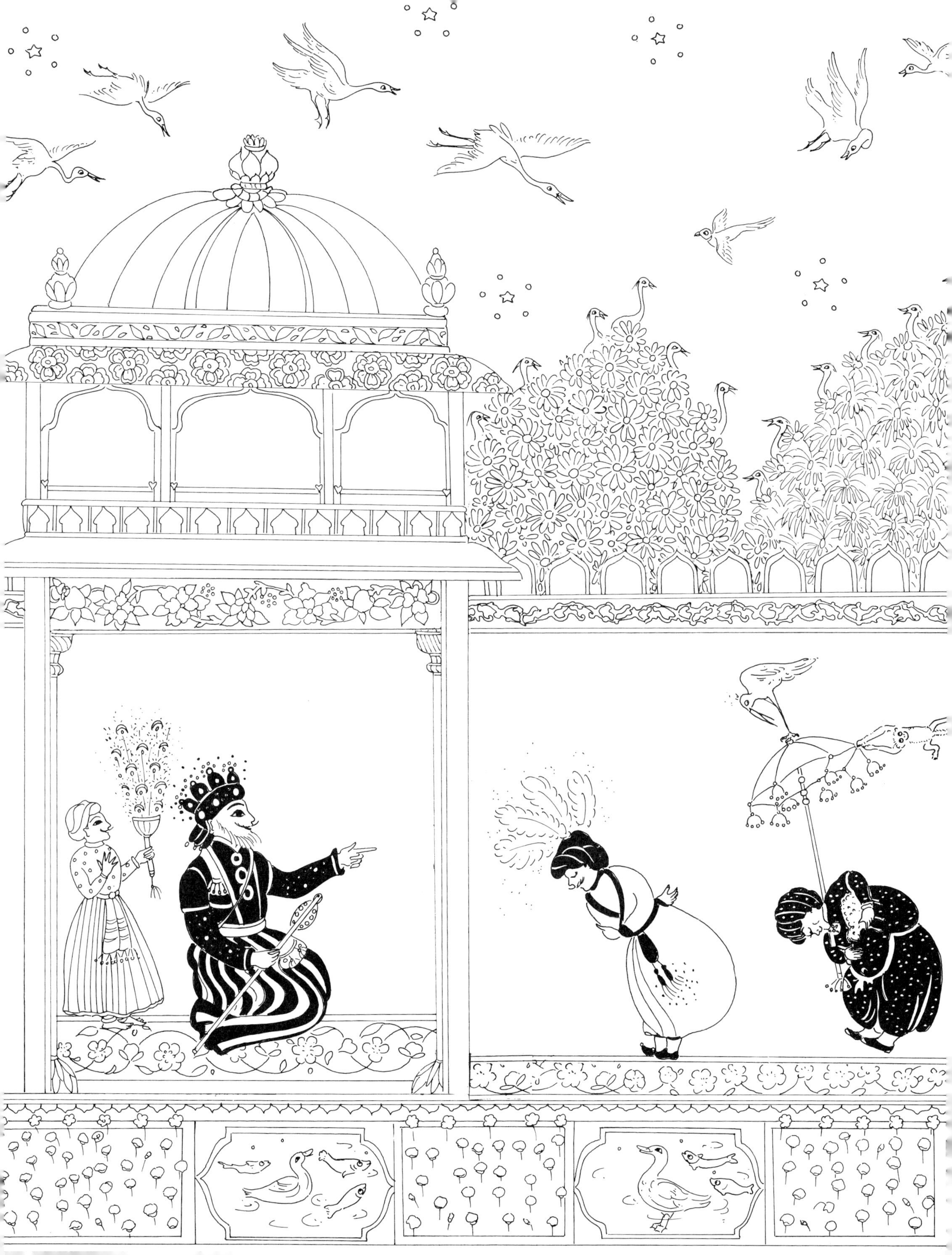

All the way home, the Maharajah worried about how he was going to carry out the Nawab's orders. He was frightened and miserable.

"What's the matter, Your Highness?" Fat Gopal kept asking. He had never seen the Maharajah looking so sad. "If you're in trouble, just tell me about it, and I'll put everything right."

"How can you help me?" the Maharajah replied at last. "You're just the court clown. The Nawab has ordered me to measure the earth from side to side and from top to bottom, to count the stars in the sky and the rays of the sun. And as if that weren't enough, he wants me to find out how many men there are in the moon. Have you ever heard of more than one? I ought to get started right away, but I don't even know how to begin."

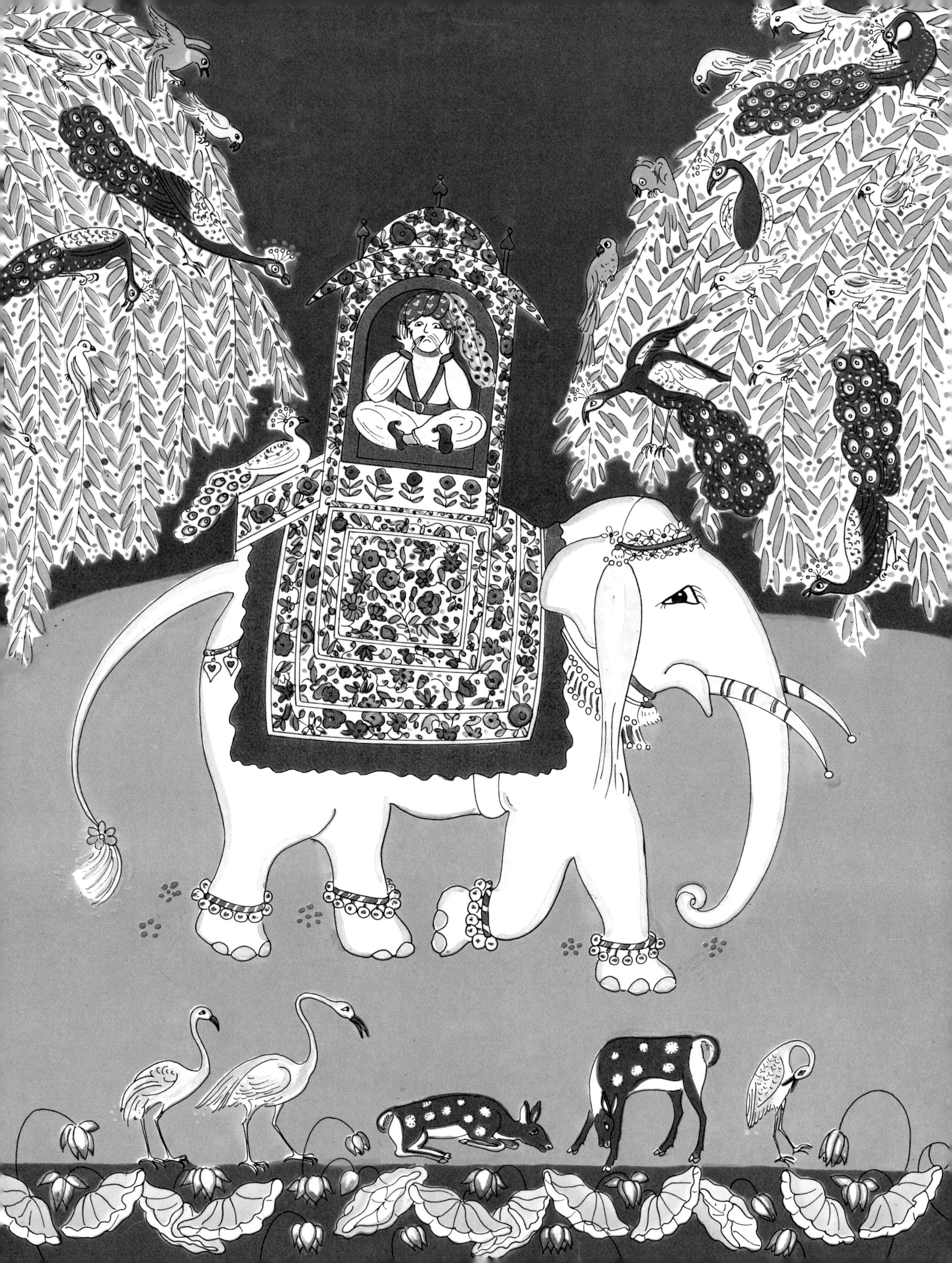

Fat Gopal's face brightened. "Not to hurry, not to worry, Your Highness," he said. "There's nothing to it. Just make me your official Star-Counter and Earth-Measurer and relax. You won't have to do a thing."

When Fat Gopal smiled, the gap between his two front teeth showed, and his eyes looked in opposite directions.

The Maharajah began to cheer up.

"Just one little favor," Fat Gopal said when he saw that the Maharajah was feeling better. "Tell the Nawab it will take a year to get the job done and will cost him a million rupees. For expenses."

The Maharajah was happy to pass the problem on to the clown. If the Nawab's orders were not carried out, perhaps it would be Fat Gopal—not he—who would lose his head.

The Nawab agreed to the terms, and for a whole year Fat Gopal had a wonderful time spending the money. He gave big parties and ate all the toasted almonds and fried cashew nuts he wanted.

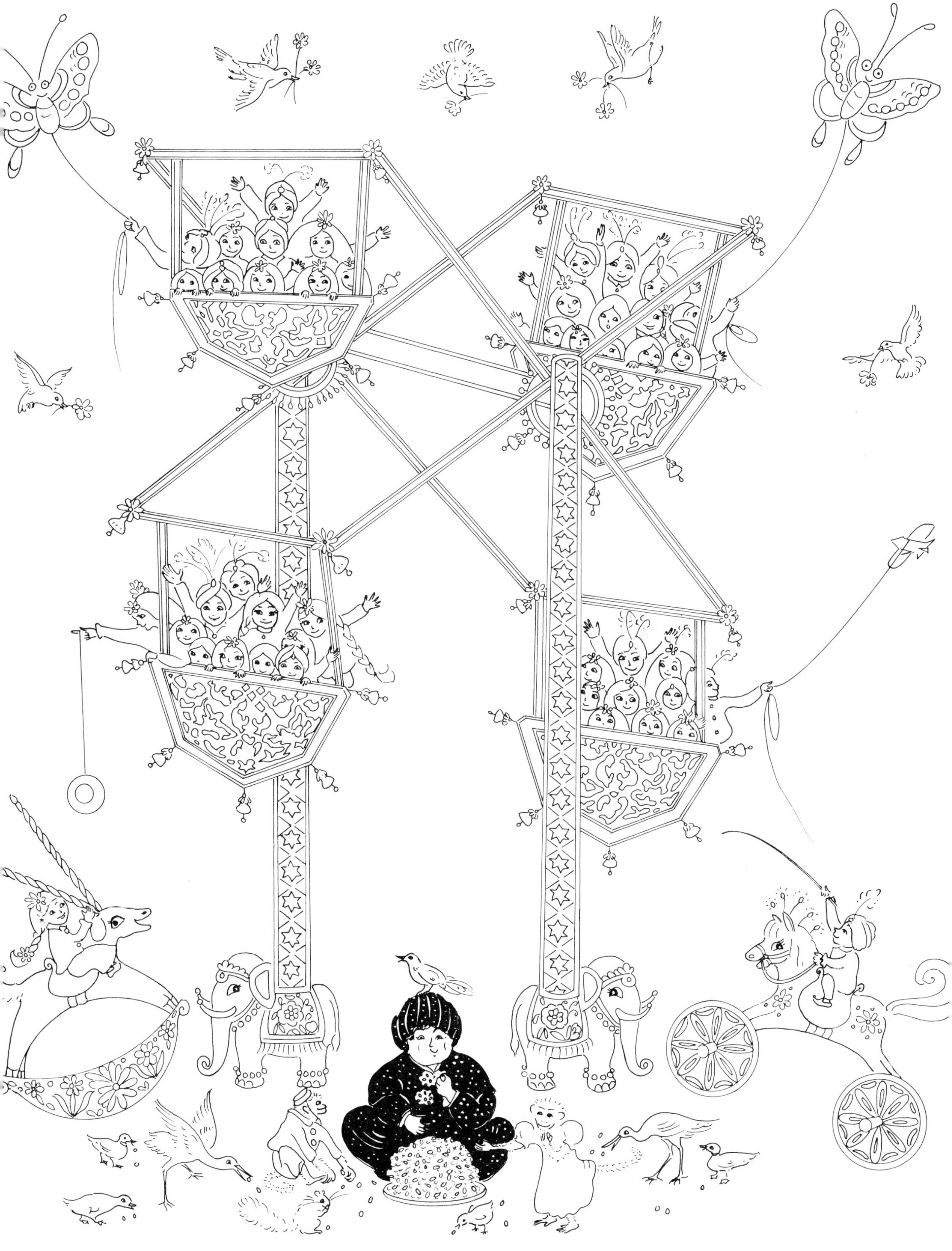

He rode around the countryside visiting his friends, sometimes on his new chariot drawn by four black horses and sometimes on a blue-eyed camel he had bought.

He hired servants to fan him with peacock feathers when it got too hot. Once he even got the Maharajah's musicians to play for him while he sat and watched the sun set behind the banana trees.

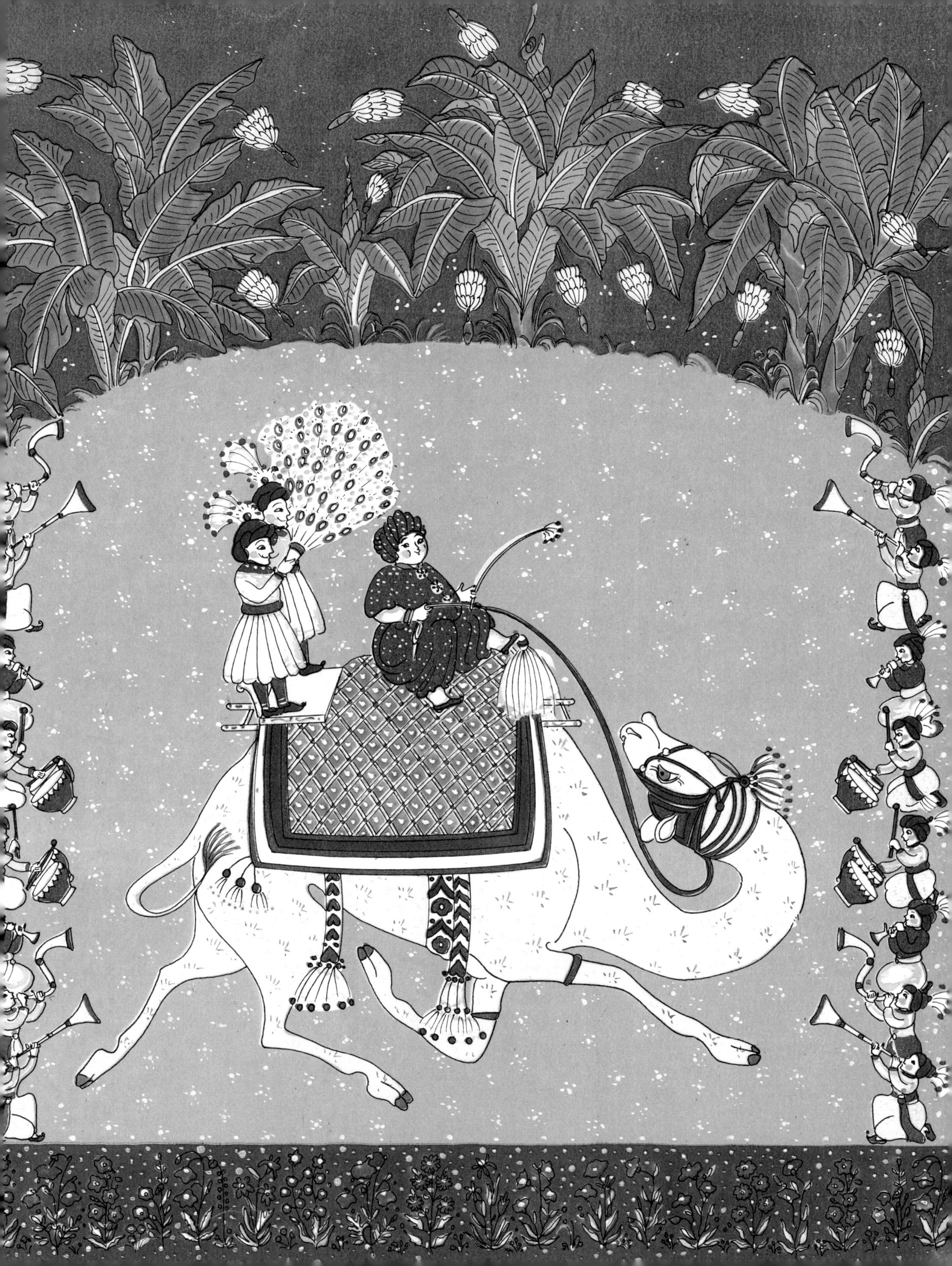

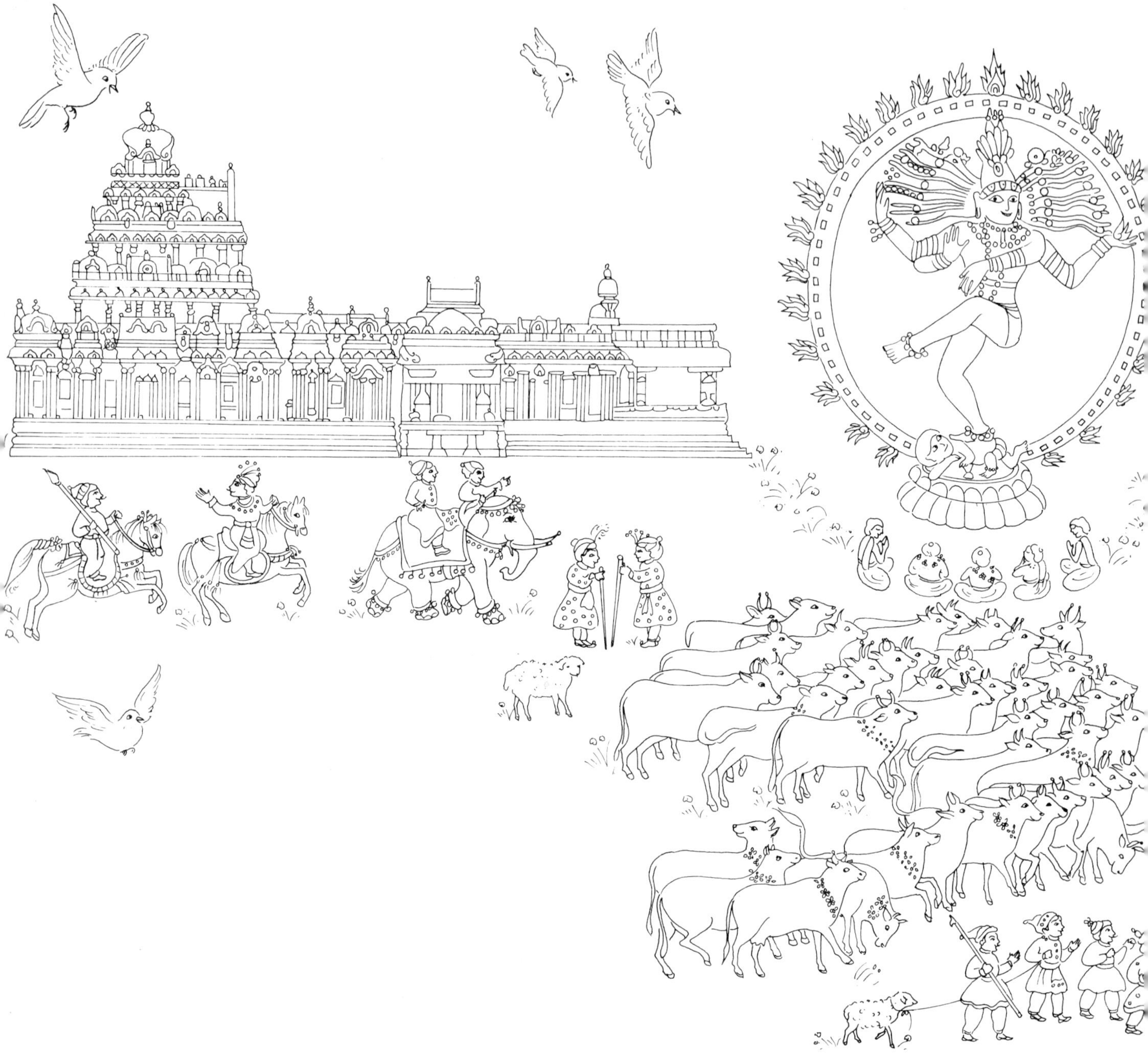

To top it all off, he went on a long trip around the whole kingdom. He was surprised to find out how fast a person can spend a million rupees.

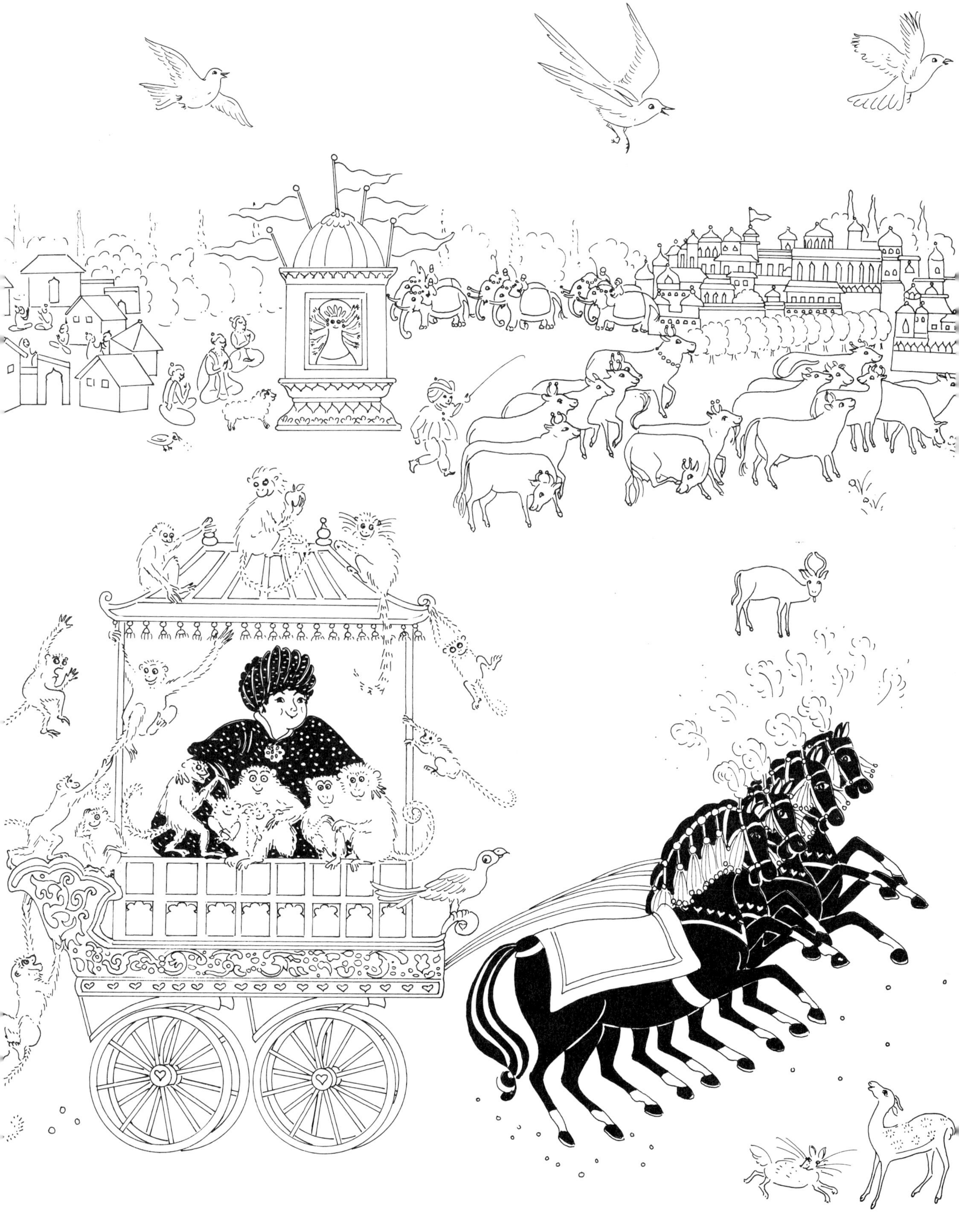

At the end of the year he went to the Maharajah's palace jingling two coins in his pocket. It was all the money he had left. He tried to look as worried as possible.

"What is it?" the Maharajah wanted to know.

"Your Highness, the job is much harder than I thought," Fat Gopal said. "I've made a start, but I must have more time. All I need is one more year—and another million rupees. For expenses. Of course, *I'll* have to be paid, too. Another million rupees when the job is finished."

The Maharajah looked doubtful. Then he remembered how excited the Nawab was about getting the earth measured, and the stars, the sun's rays, and the men in the moon counted. "I'll see what I can do," he said to Fat Gopal. And he did. He got the Nawab to agree to everything.

"Not to hurry, not to worry," Fat Gopal said as he set out once again.

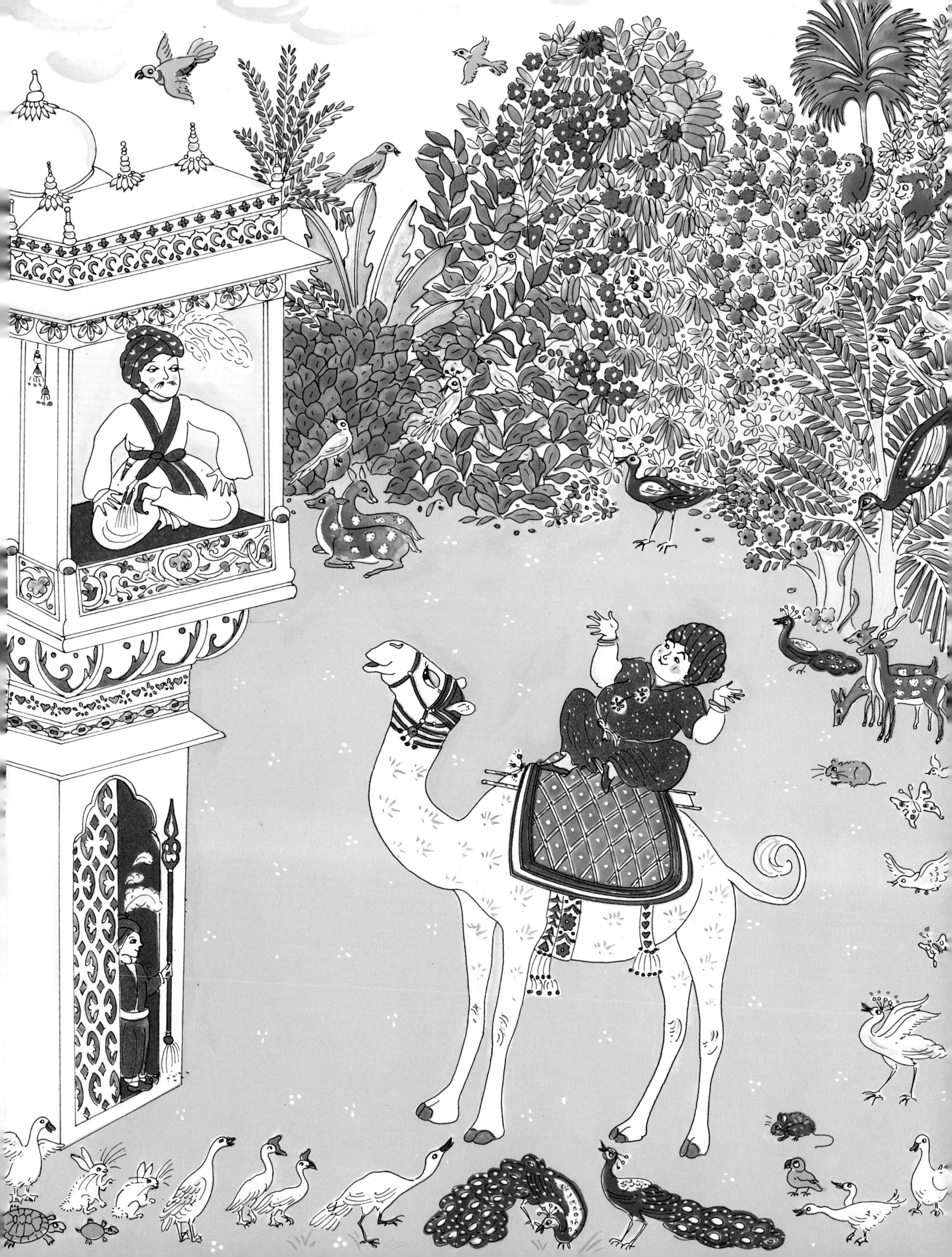

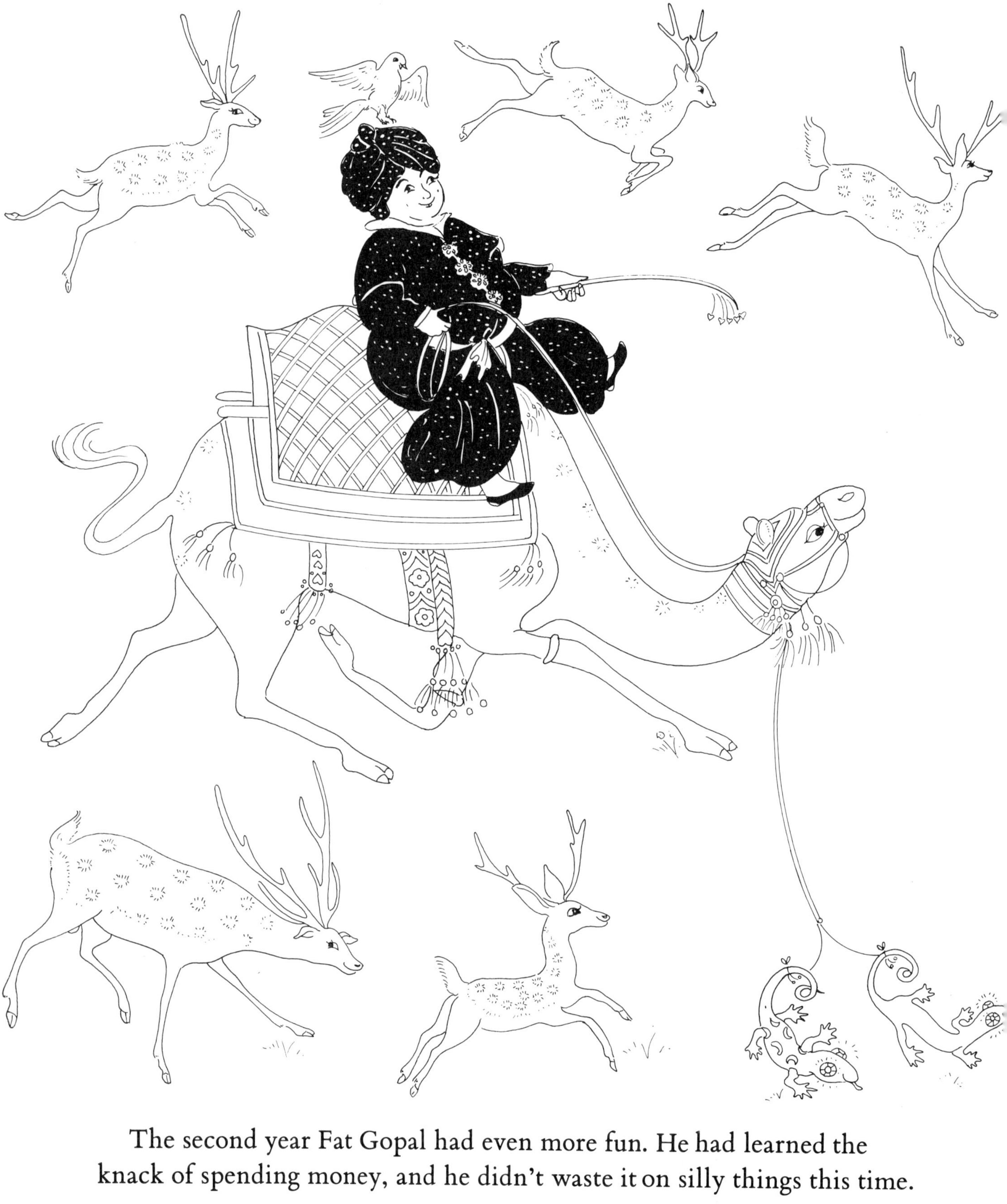

The second year Fat Gopal had even more fun. He had learned the knack of spending money, and he didn't waste it on silly things this time.

He bought a pet tiger, a pair of
lizards with diamond eyes,
and a dozen deer with
golden antlers.

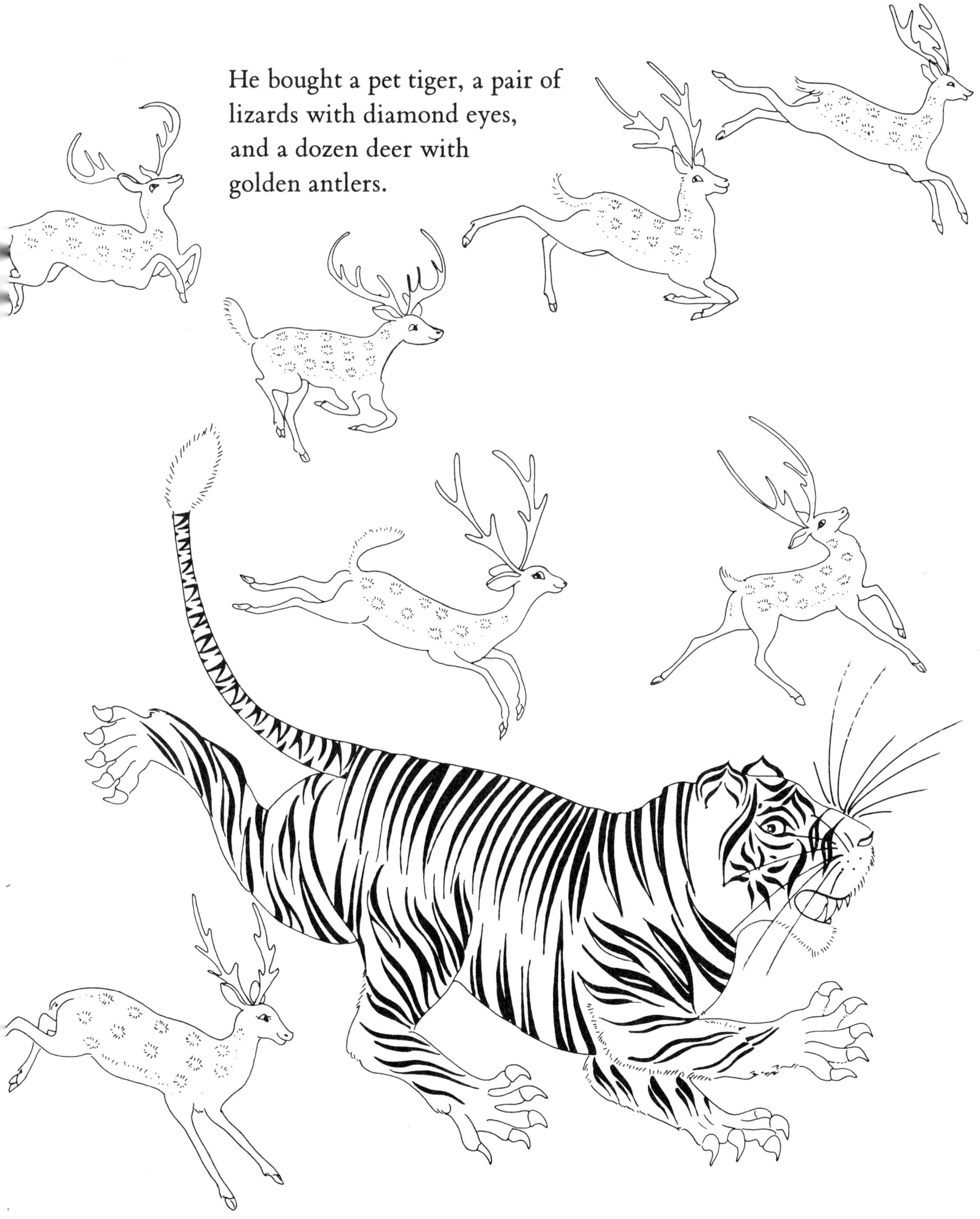

He traded his blue-eyed camel for a boat with red sails and took his friends for a ride on the river every evening. He treated them to spiced tea and creamy white fudge with pistachio nuts. Before he knew it, his second year was up and his second million rupees spent.

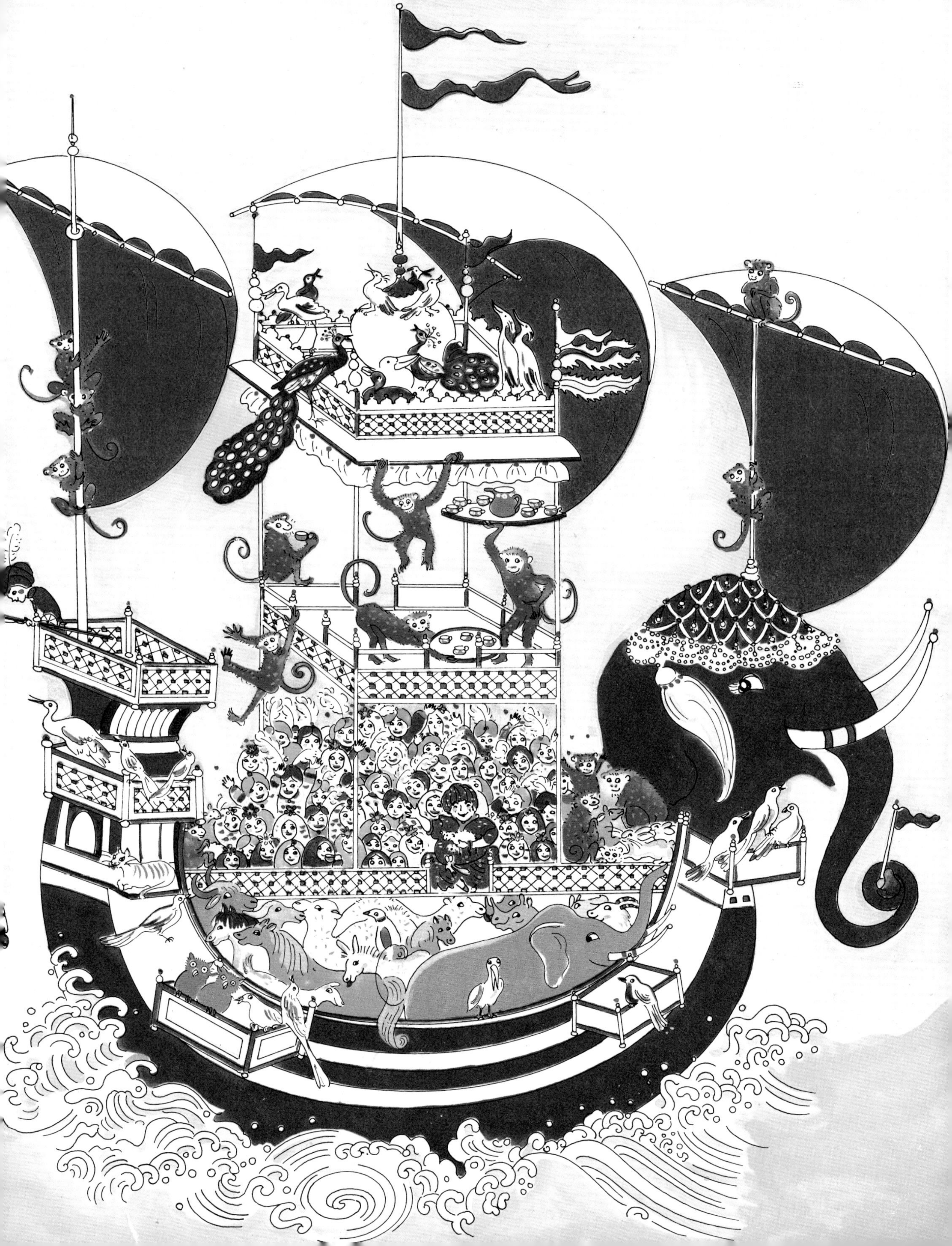

He arrived just in time at the Nawab's palace with eight wooden carts pulled by bullocks. They were overflowing with bundles of thread, all tangled and knotted and stuffed in every which way. Behind the bullock carts strutted five peacocks. Behind them were ten men carrying baskets that contained something mysterious. Last came two tigers in cages. They were *not* pet tigers.

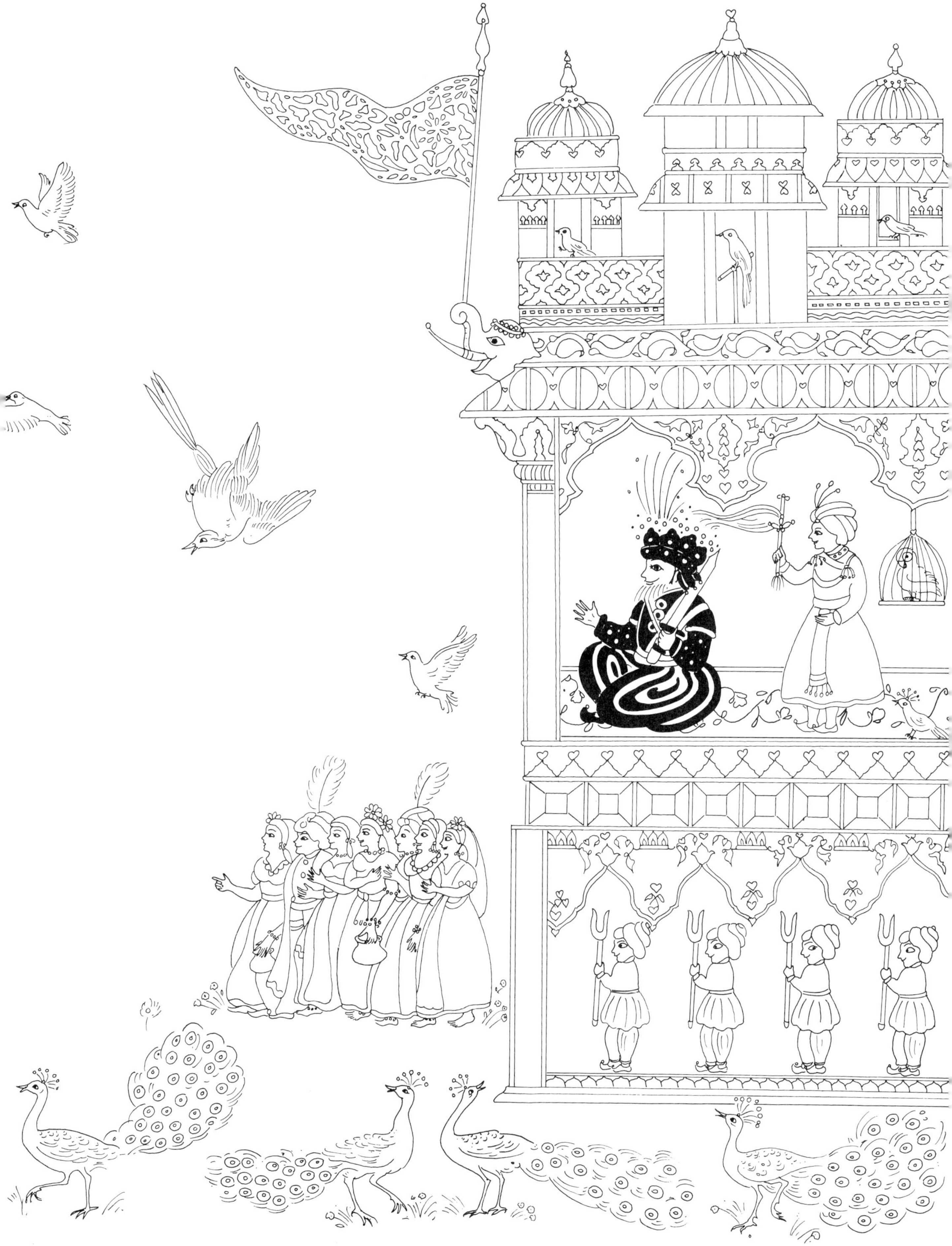

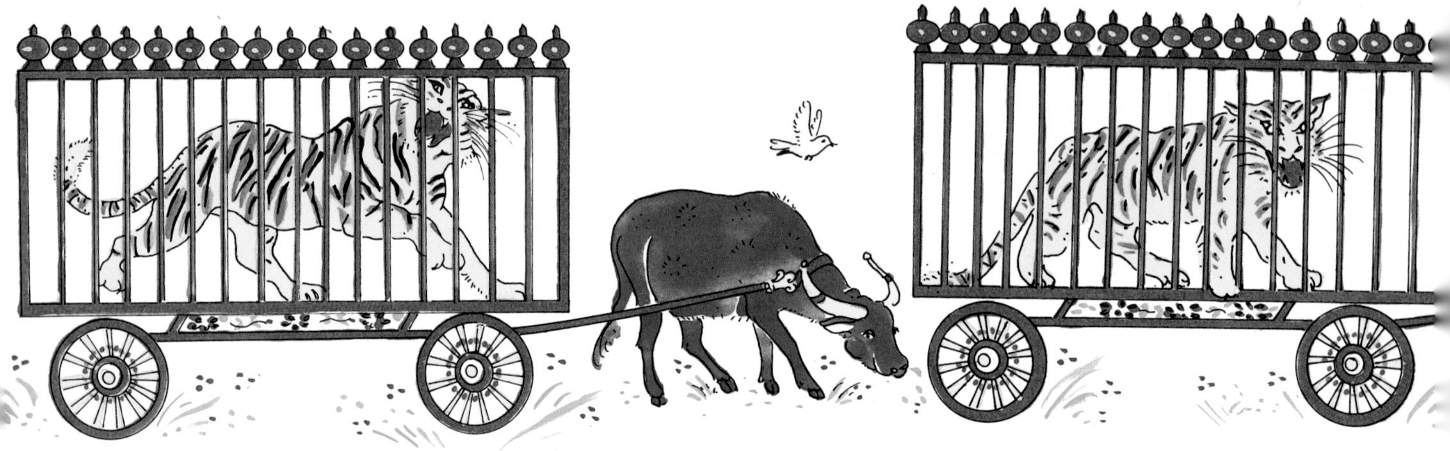

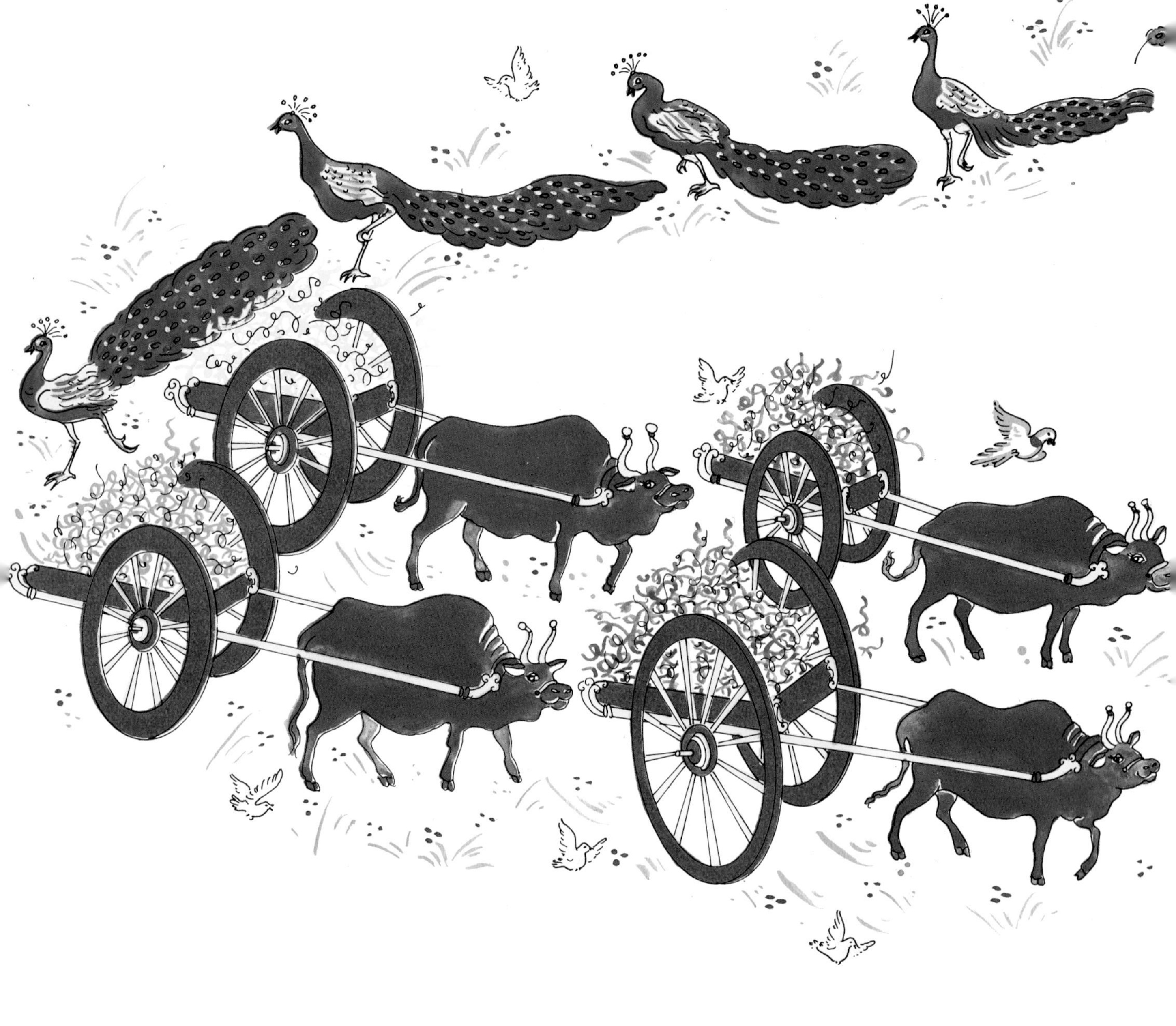

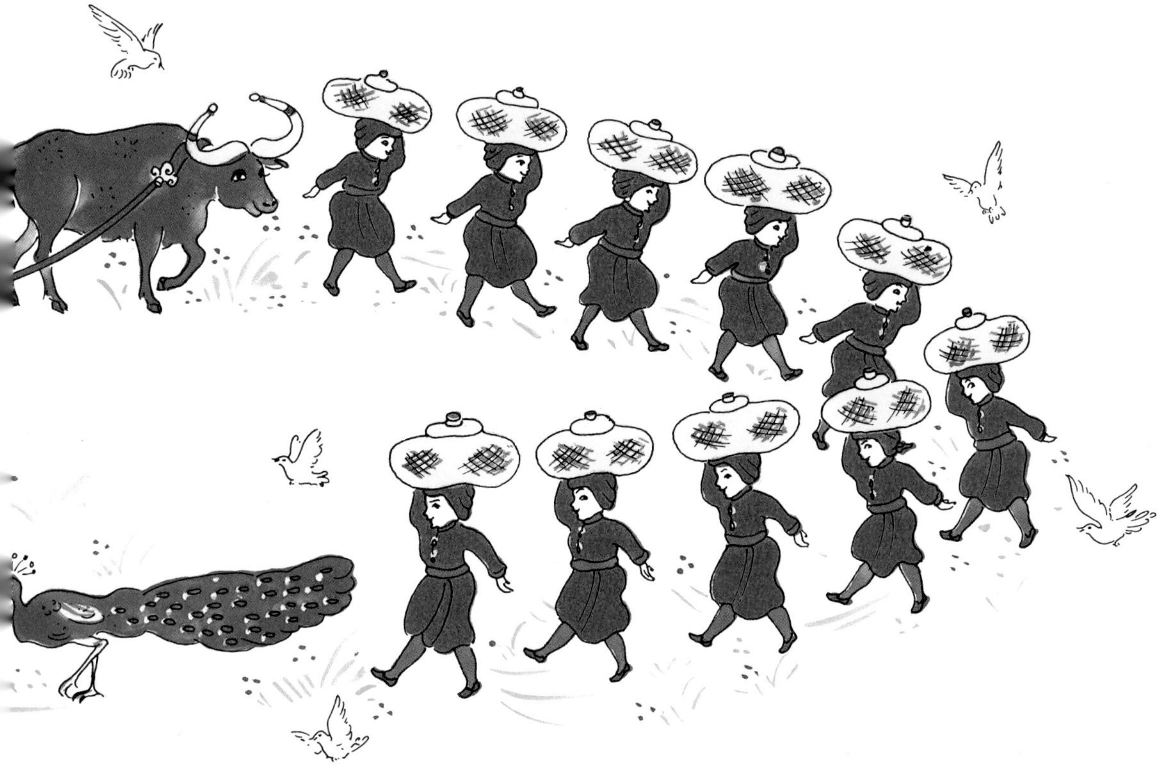

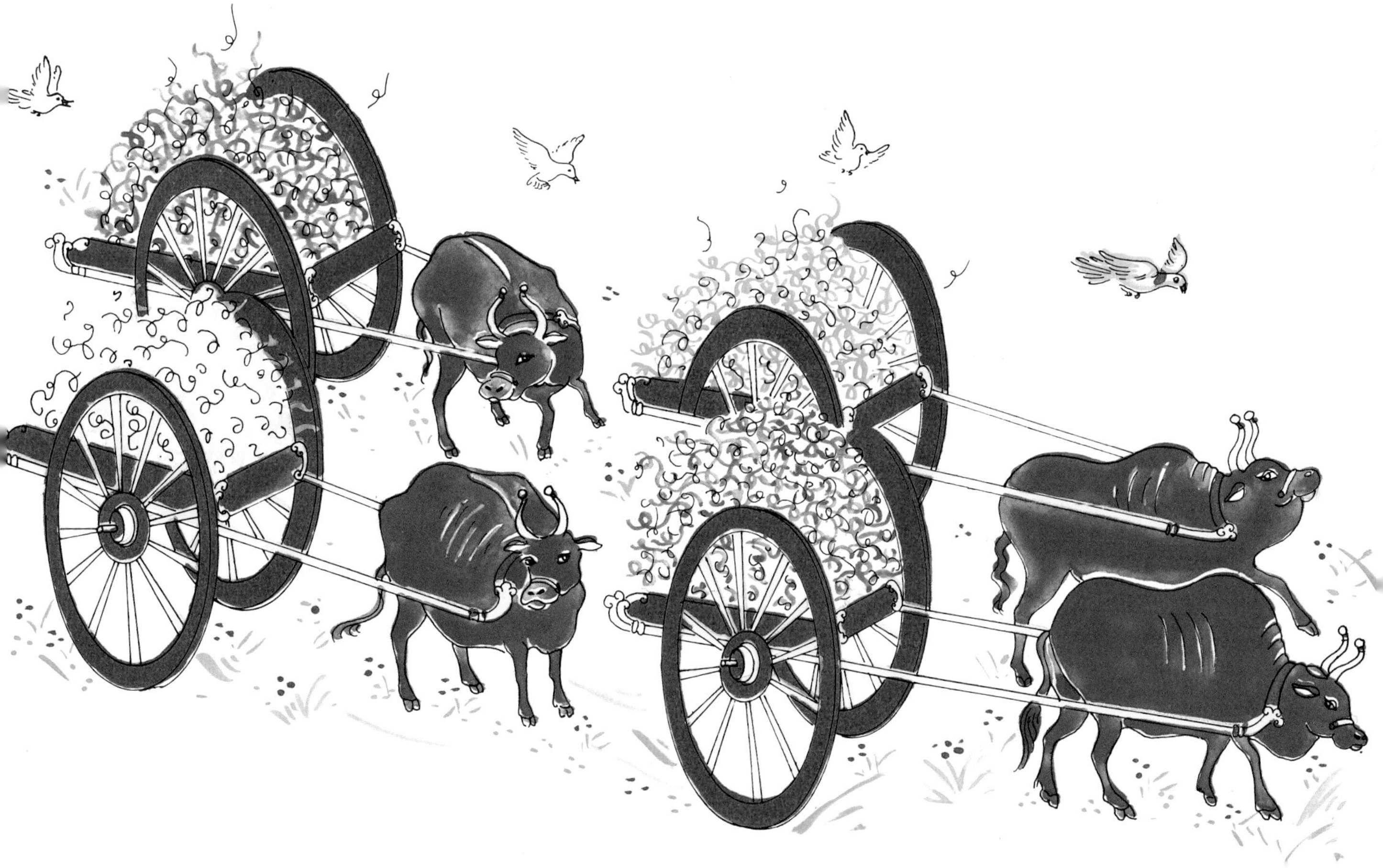

"Your Majesty," Fat Gopal said, bowing low before the Nawab, "I have measured the earth from end to end and top to bottom, counted the stars in the sky and the rays of the sun. I have also found out how many men there are in the moon."

"That's marvelous," the Nawab exclaimed. "Worth waiting two years for. Now give me the figures. The figures, I say!"

"Figures, Your Majesty?" Fat Gopal said. His eyes opened wide in surprise. "If you'll excuse me for reminding you, giving the figures was not part of the job. I was just supposed to count and measure, measure and count, and that I have done."

Fat Gopal then told the Nawab that the earth, measured from end to end, was as wide as the thread in the first five bullock carts was long. Measured from top to bottom, the earth was as long as the thread in the remaining three bullock carts. "Just see for yourself, Your Majesty," he said.

"As for the stars in the sky," he went on, "there are as many as there are feathers on these peacocks. And believe me, I had a hard time finding birds with just the right number of feathers."

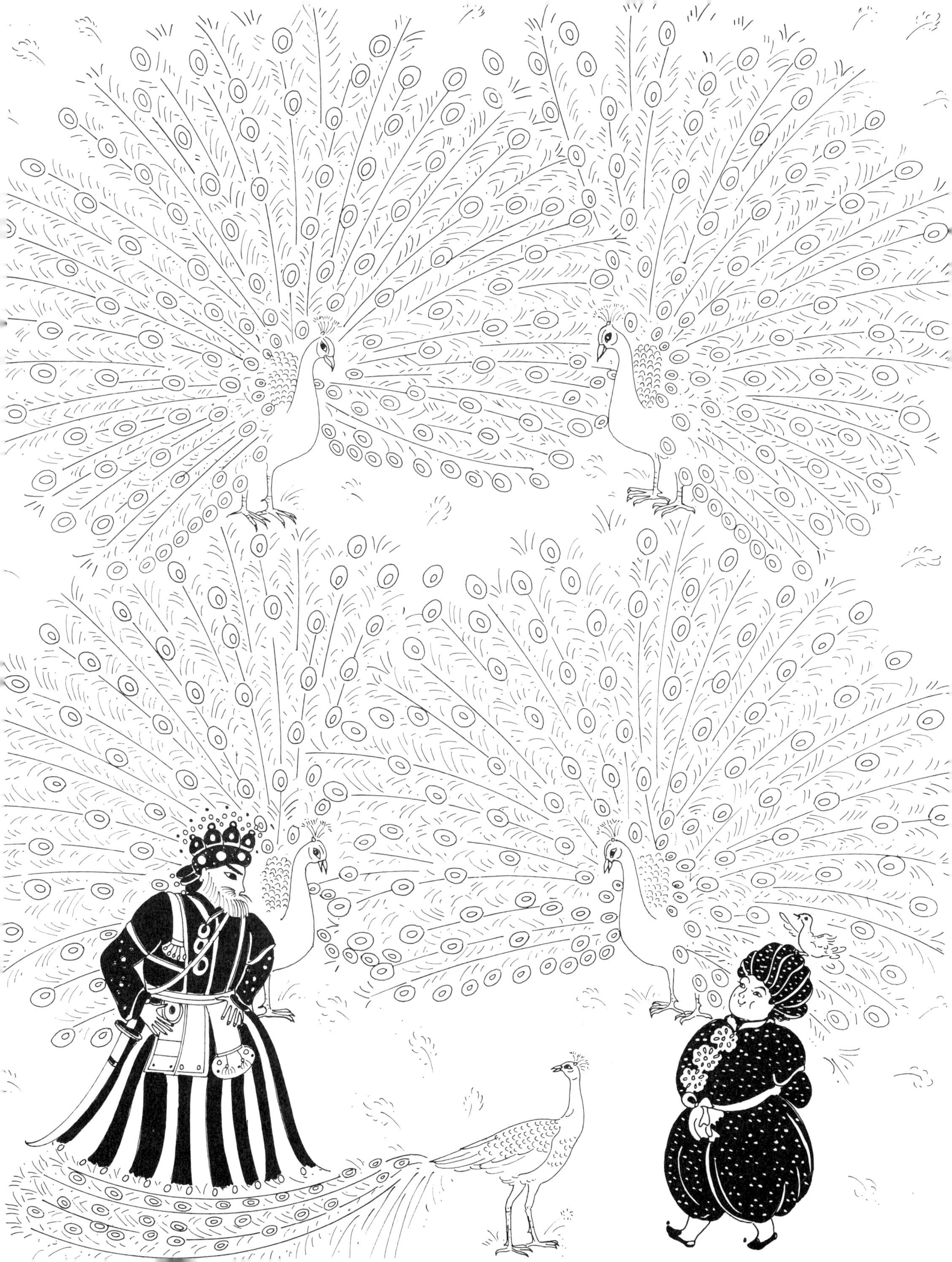

Next, Fat Gopal lifted the lids from the mysterious baskets. "The sun has as many rays as these have scales," he said brightly as some angry-looking snakes raised their heads and flicked out their tongues. "And there are as many men in the moon as these tigers have hairs on their backs."

It was the Nawab's turn to be flabbergasted. "I can't measure that thread or count those peacock feathers. And I'm not going to count the scales on the snakes, either." Then he stared at the tigers in the cages. They growled back. "You don't expect me to see how many hairs they have on their backs, do you?" he shouted.

Fat Gopal didn't say anything. He just stood in front of the Nawab with his head bowed, trying to look as respectful as possible.

The Nawab sat back, blinked a couple of times, and slowly shook his head. Finally he said, "I have to admit I asked you to measure and count, count and measure, and you have done it."

"Yes, Your Majesty," Fat Gopal said. He stole a quick look at the Nawab. "Now, about my pay . . ."

The Nawab frowned. After a long time he said, "You shall have your money. I never break a promise."

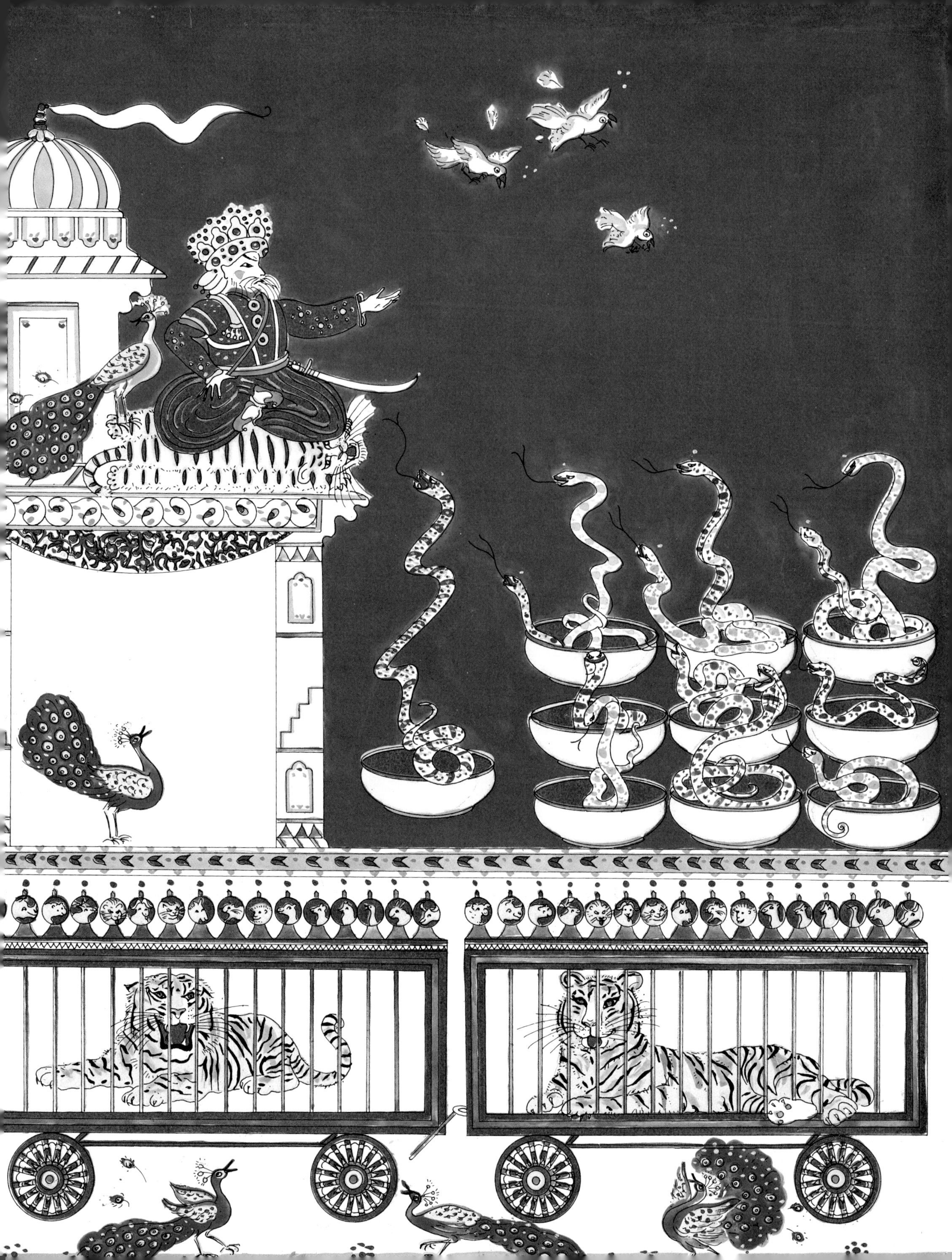

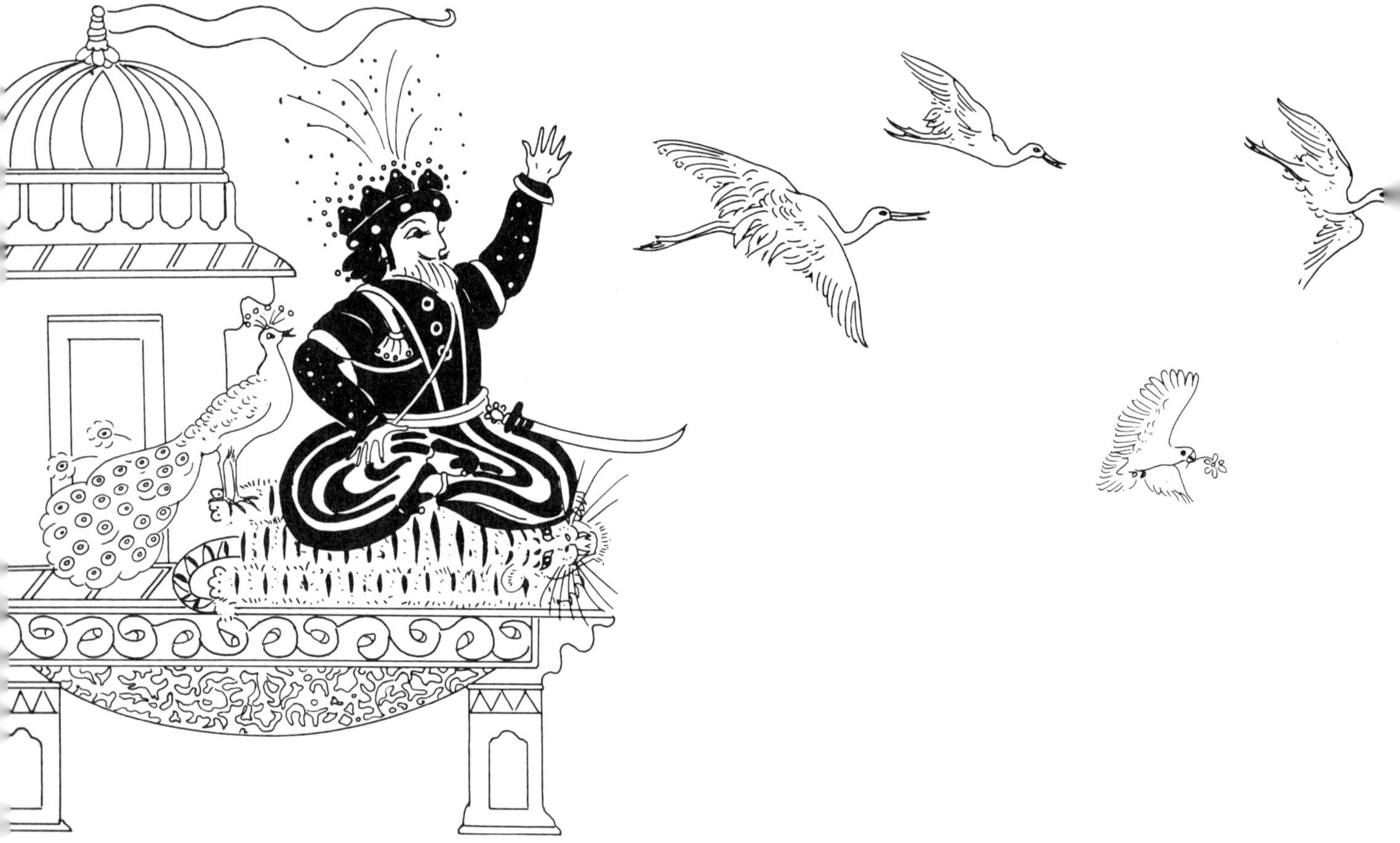

Without waiting a minute, he ordered his servants to bring another million rupees from the big room in the palace where he kept all his treasure.

"Here," the Nawab said, as if throwing a coin to a beggar. Then with a wave of his hand, he told Fat Gopal to go. After a moment he called him back. "For good measure, you might as well take one of the elephants from my herd." He said it as if he had too many elephants and didn't know what to do with them all. "But don't let me see you in my palace again!"

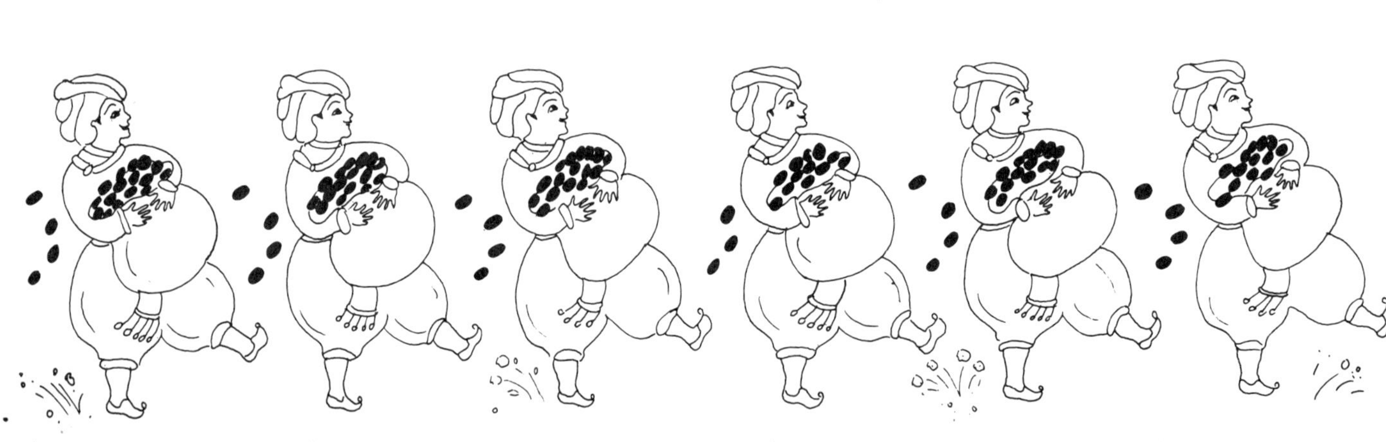

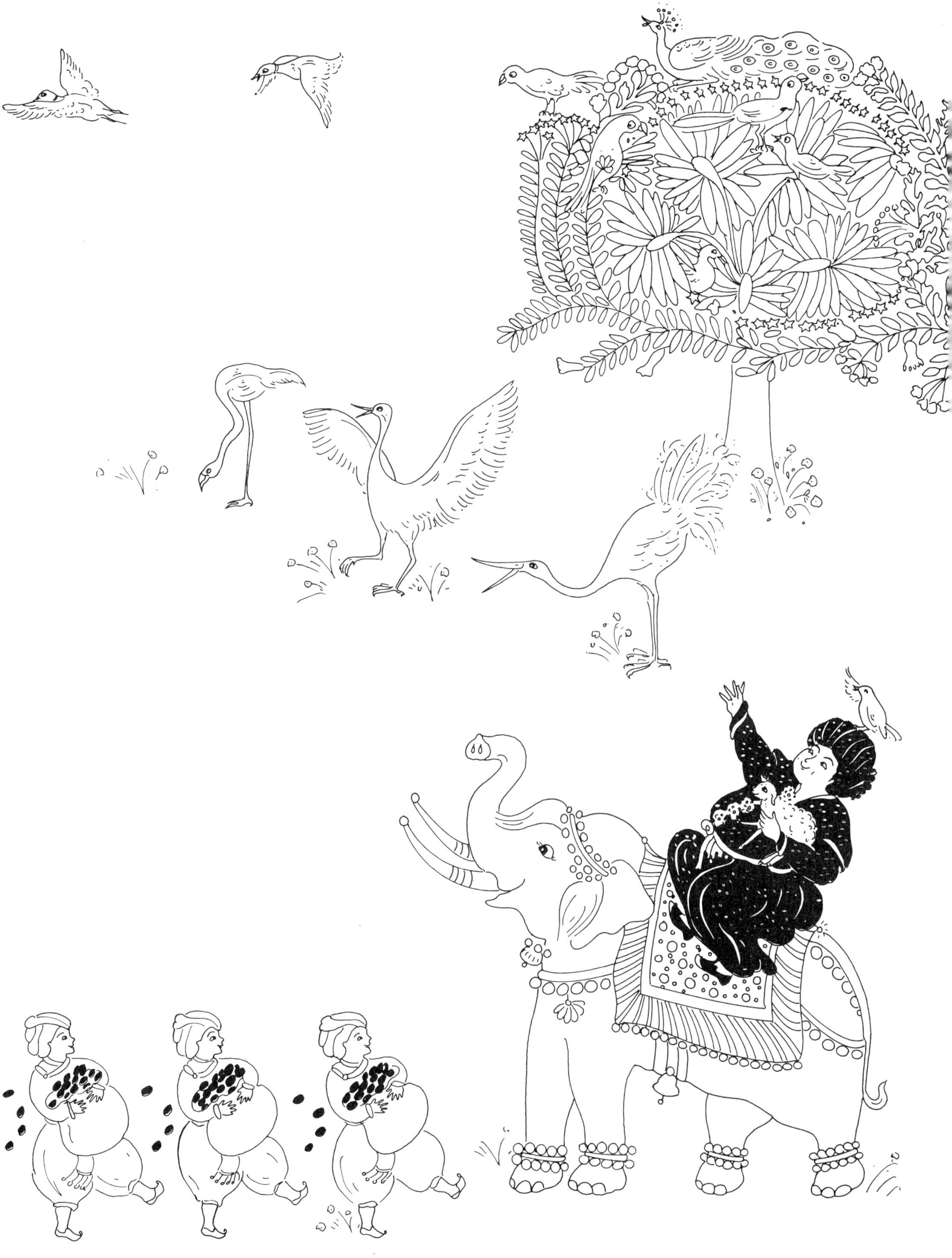

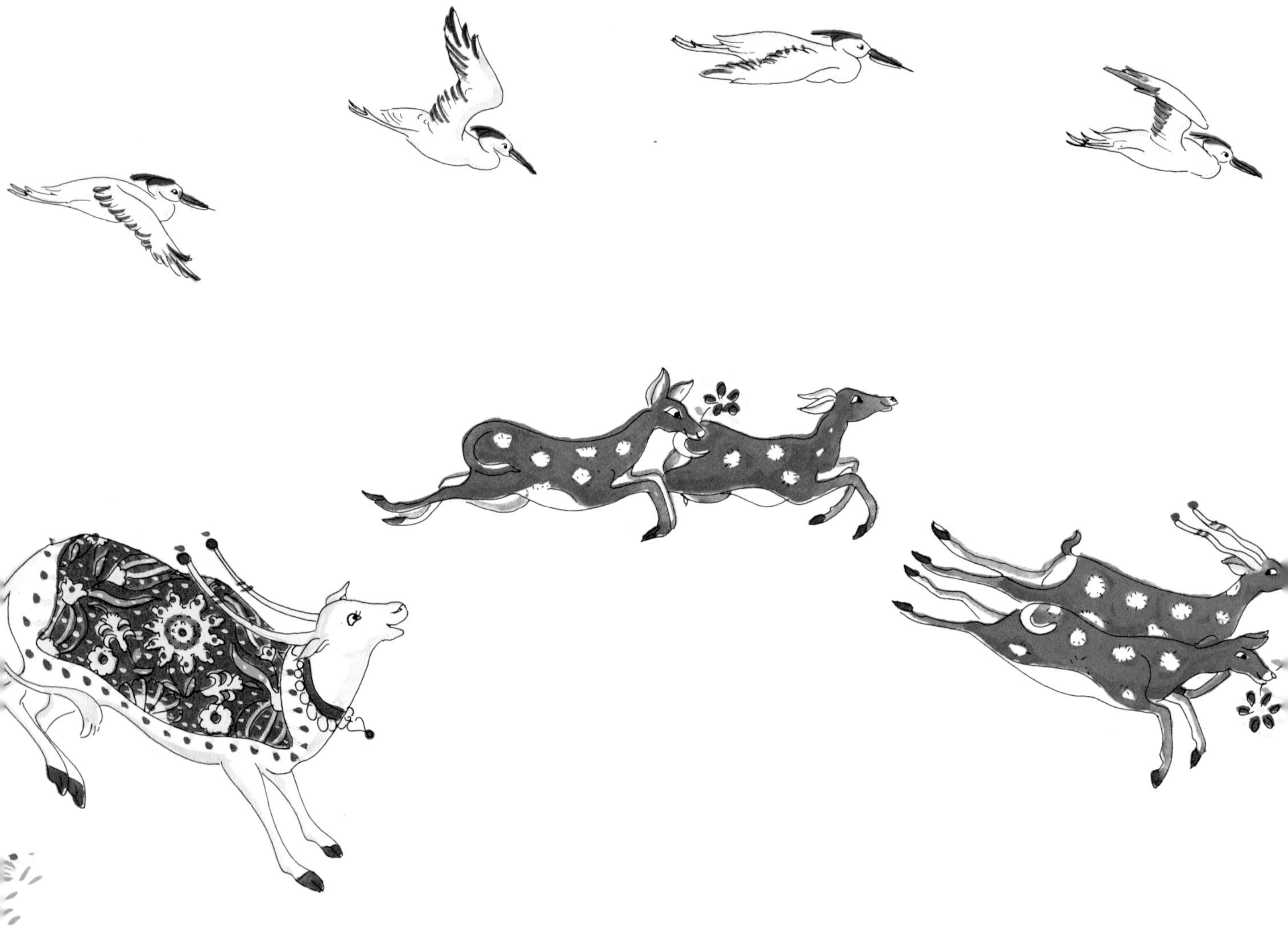

Fat Gopal rode off with a big smile on his face. The gap in his front teeth showed, and his eyes looked in opposite directions. He didn't mind if the elephant was not exactly the best. He was already figuring out how he would spend his third million rupees.

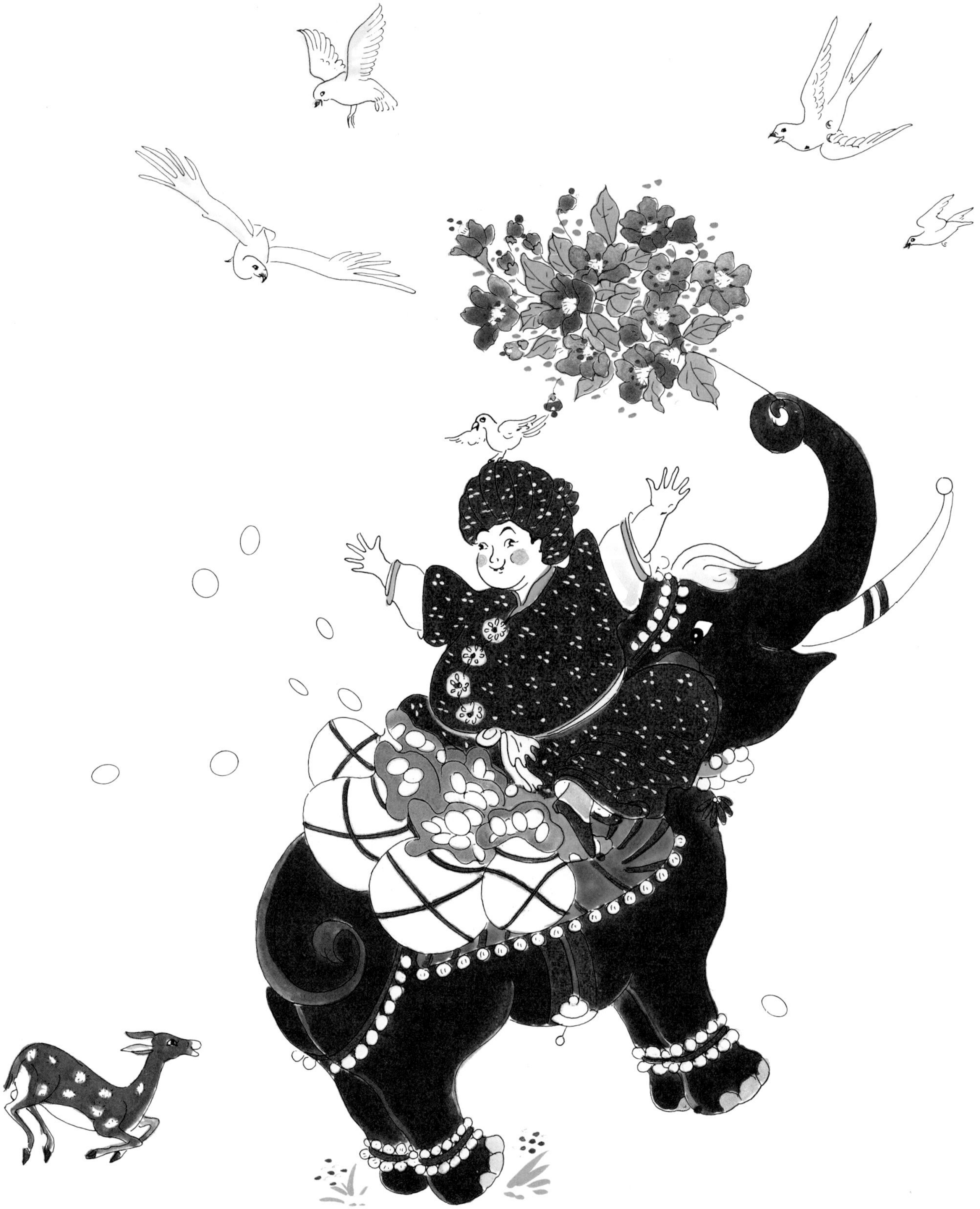

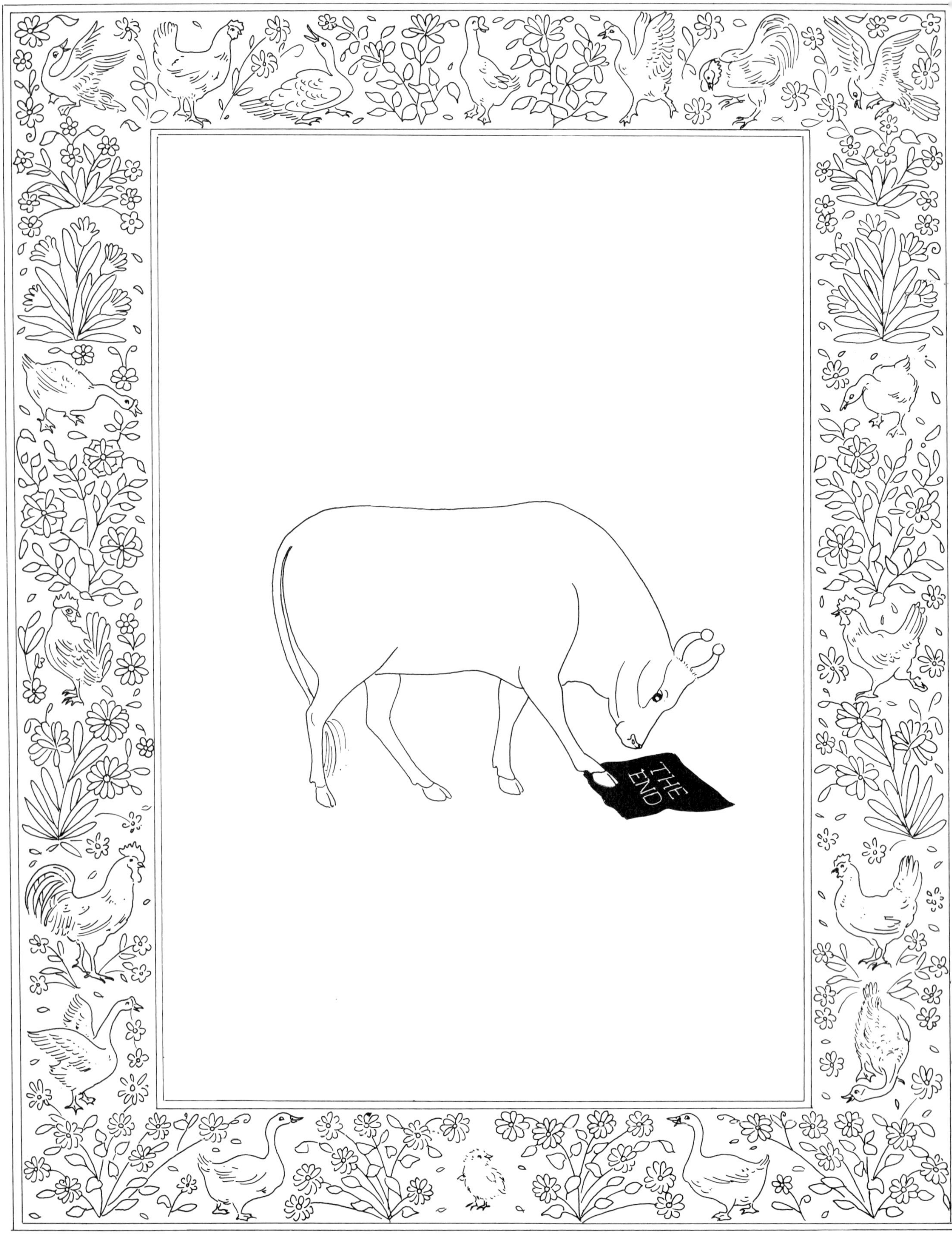
THE
END

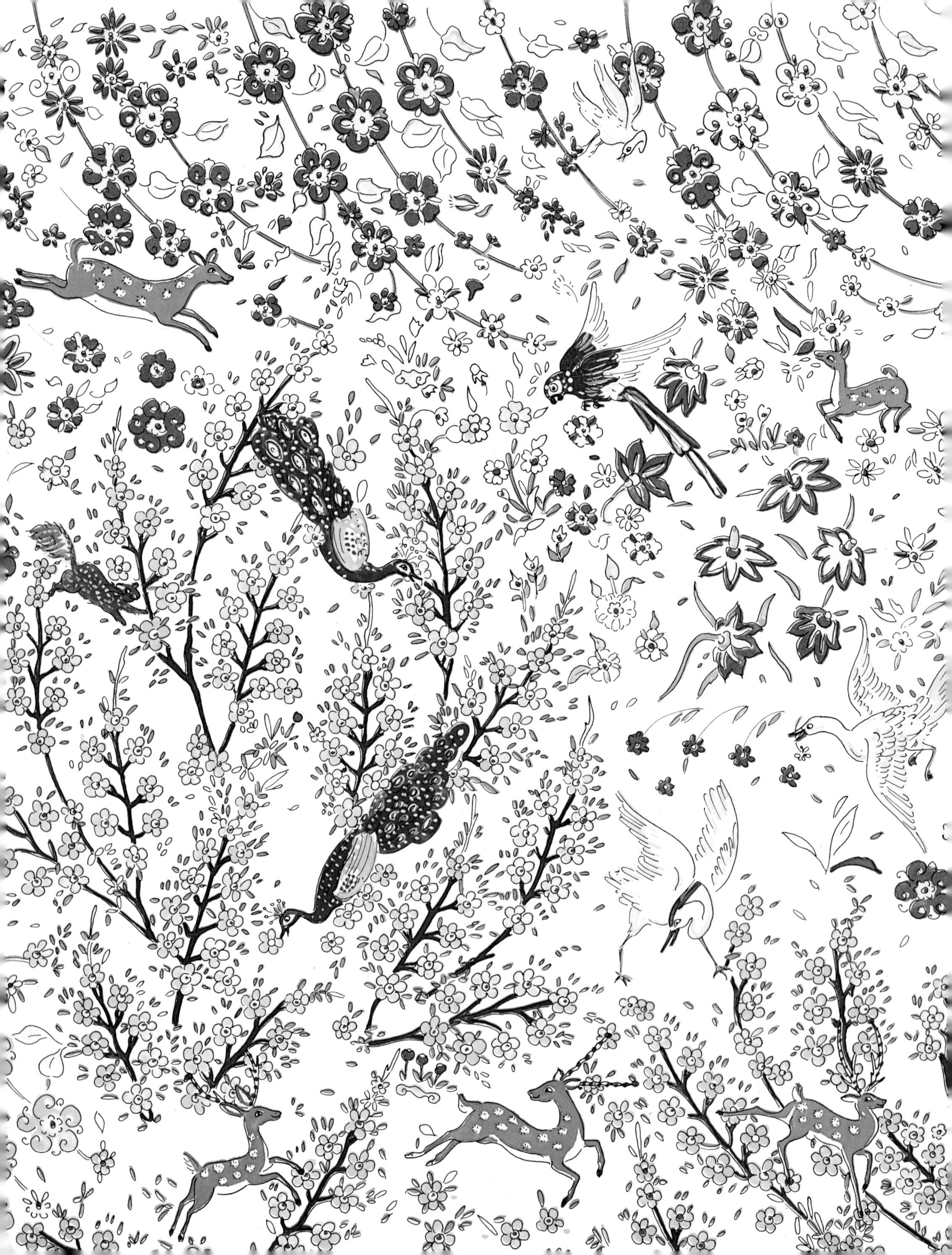

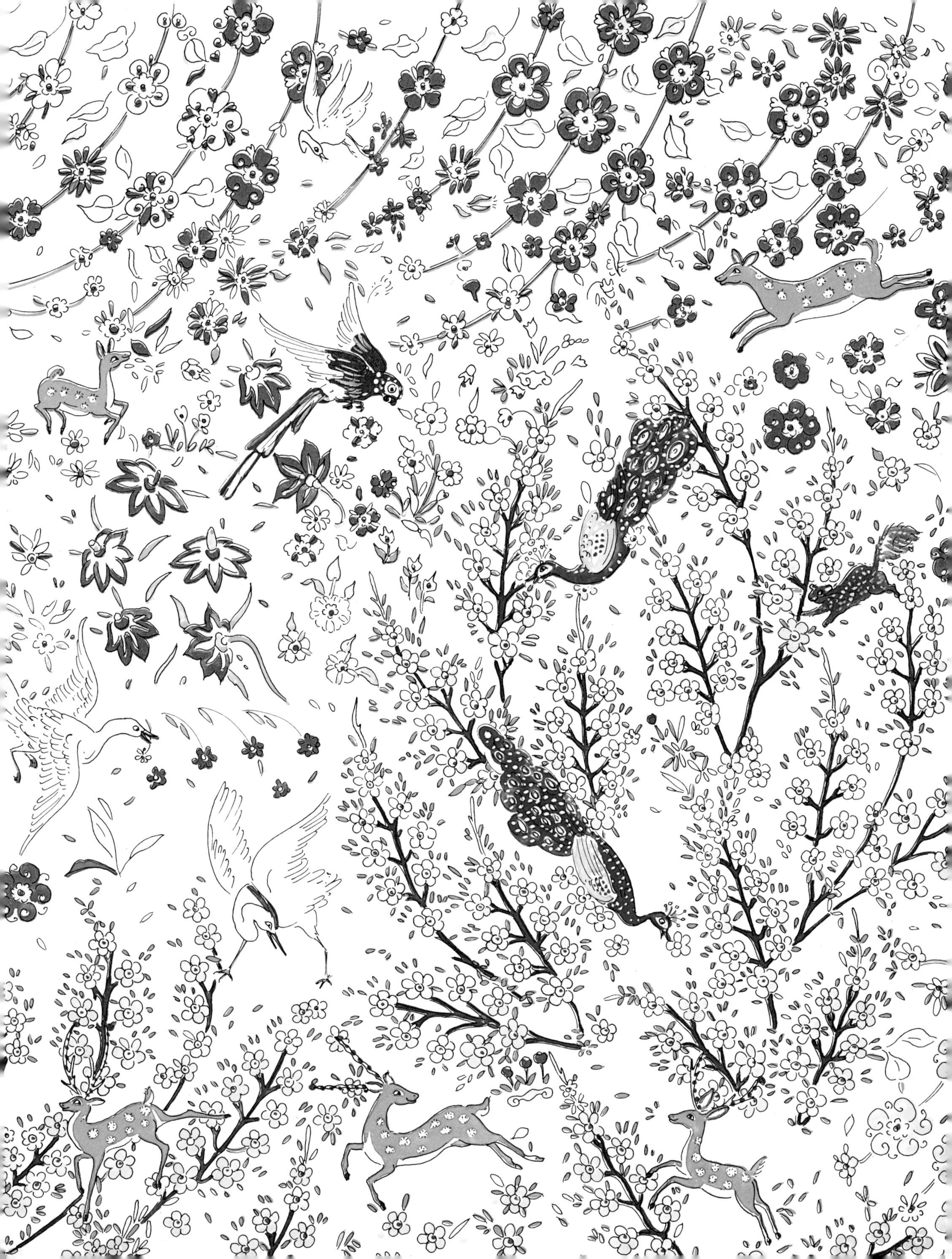